Persuading the Earl

The Country House Romantic Mysteries
Book 1

by
Audrey Harrison

© Copyright 2023 by Audrey Harrison
Text by Audrey Harrison
Cover by Kim Killion

Dragonblade Publishing, Inc. is an imprint of Kathryn Le Veque Novels, Inc.
P.O. Box 23
Moreno Valley, CA 92556
ceo@dragonbladepublishing.com

Produced in the United States of America

First Edition May 2023
Print Edition

Reproduction of any kind except where it pertains to short quotes in relation to advertising or promotion is strictly prohibited.

All Rights Reserved.

The characters and events portrayed in this book are fictitious. Any similarity to real persons, living or dead, is purely coincidental and not intended by the author.

Find more about the author and contact details at the end of this book and the chance to obtain a free copy of The Unwilling Earl.

ARE YOU SIGNED UP FOR DRAGONBLADE'S BLOG?

You'll get the latest news and information on exclusive giveaways, exclusive excerpts, coming releases, sales, free books, cover reveals and more.

Check out our complete list of authors, too!

No spam, no junk. That's a promise!

Sign Up Here

www.dragonbladepublishing.com

Dearest Reader;

Thank you for your support of a small press. At Dragonblade Publishing, we strive to bring you the highest quality Historical Romance from some of the best authors in the business. Without your support, there is no 'us', so we sincerely hope you adore these stories and find some new favorite authors along the way.

Happy Reading!

CEO, Dragonblade Publishing

Chapter One

Hampshire, 1811

"Aunt, I have told you a hundred times that I will not marry, and you know very well why not," Richard Fox, Earl of Douglas, said with a pained expression.

"It is long past time you were wed; you have responsibilities to the continuation of your heritage."

"That is hardly a fact to encourage me to marry, even if I was willing to do so, and as I am not, it just adds to the long list of reasons why I am right in my decision."

"You are flawed in every argument, you foolish boy. You are letting the past influence your future, and those are the actions of a ninnyhammer."

"I am the ninnyhammer? You are the one who threatened that you were determined to find me a wife, and now you are filling the house with spinsters who no one else wants. I am minded to predict that your scheme is doomed to fail before it has started, which I am more than happy about."

"I have invited those who I thought would suit you. I hope you give them a chance."

"Why should I raise expectations in women who have been unable to find a match elsewhere? I would expect at least one of the diamonds of the Season to be in attendance," Richard drawled to his aunt. He stood in the large drawing room of his aunt's house, one hand gripping the back of a chair, the other holding his quizzing glass to his eye, which had made many a lesser person wither under his scrutiny.

"Any more of that insolence and I will box your ears, my boy," Marie responded, not in the slightest daunted that her nephew was looking at her with his usual disdainful expression, his cold blue eyes challenging her.

There was a slight pause, but then Richard laughed, tucking his glass into his waistcoat pocket. "My apologies, Aunt. I have spent too long in London with the wrong set, and I forget myself until I settle back in to country life, but when you try to meddle, it brings out the worst in me."

"Pfft, you are the leader of the wrong set if the gossip is even half true," Marie said, fixing her skirts around her in a more comfortable manner. She still preferred the older style of apparel rather than the modern empire line dresses; her formal attire made her even more intimidating, supported by the disdainful expressions which were a trait of her family.

"You should not believe everything you read in those pamphlets. They make their money by spreading exaggerated stories." Richard defended himself, but the smile that accompanied the words undermined his suggestion of innocence.

"That might be the case with regard to some of your friends, but I know you too well. The stories have more than a ring of truth about them."

Richard laughed at his aunt, the usual dark expression which marred his otherwise handsome features gone for the moment at least. She was the only person who could make him fully relax and be himself, and even that happened rarely. "I should never have told you half of what I relayed. I was young and foolish when I began this blasted practice of confessing everything to you, and I cannot stop the habit. It is too tempting when I know you will find it as funny as I do when I recount my escapades."

"Yes, you have always been eager to tell me all your exploits, but it is time you settled down, though I have noticed that you have become even more difficult to please. I am left with mothers of disappointed daughters telling me their woes of how they were sure you were about to propose to their daughter."

"Not a chance in hell would I give the slightest hint I was interested in marriage to anyone I had the misfortune to be introduced to; the stories about my attachment to any chit are most definitely exaggerated. It is far too dangerous to start up a flirtation with an innocent when there are schemers who abound in society. Dancing with them is bad enough; I can feel expectant eyes boring into me, trying to work out if there shall be a proposal."

"I am surprised they would contemplate such a thing; you always look as if you are about to be led to the gallows whenever you are in a ballroom."

"Are you surprised? I am tortured with chits who can barely string a sentence together and who have clearly been instructed in the so-called art of flirting. When they bat their eyelashes at me, I can honestly say that, in most cases, I am reminded of a camel with the way they tilt their heads and smile. It is damned off-putting."

Marie ignored the language her nephew used; she was used to his lack of restraint in her company and welcomed it. He had been a lonely boy with no one to turn to after the death of his mother until she had forced herself into his life, though her brother, Richard's father, had been against her interference.

Her brother's dismissal of her would have been enough for most people to abandon the child, but Marie was not most people, and she had given her brother enough of a roasting that he gave in and accepted she would be Richard's main carer. The new set-up suited nephew and aunt perfectly and allowed Richard to experience some form of happiness once more, though he was always a little aloof from everyone, even Marie at times. But then something had happened that reinforced his conviction that he was easily discarded, and he had changed for the worse since then.

"I thought that would be your opinion on the matter and told them exactly that. They are bigger fools if they think I would persuade you to marry any silly girl, whether she is considered the catch of the Season or not."

Richard grinned at her. "I love you."

"In that case, stop being a brute and welcome everyone I have invited with grace. It is time you forgot the past."

His expression turned dark once more. "How could I?"

"She chose someone else. Yes, I think she was a fool to do so, but it does not alter the fact. Do not let her fickleness spoil your future happiness."

Richard turned to the window, refusing to let even his aunt see the distress in his expression. The person he had thought could finally wipe away the pain of the past had gone on to reinforce his insecurity about being easily abandoned and unlovable. "Every time I go to London, I see her. She visits me regularly and always wants us to dance and be included in my plans. I have not the will to refuse her anything."

"Then you are a bigger gudgeon than she is. If you believe that by behaving the way you do and remaining unwed, she will regret her decision and be longing for you, then you are very much mistaken."

The words had the effect of lifting his lips slightly, but his eyes were filled with anguish. "I do not know what I am trying to prove to her or myself, but I cannot break away from her, though it chips away at my insides every time I see her. I have considered going to the continent to try to deaden the pain of being in her company. It is that or I drink myself into a stupor enough times that one day I will just not wake up."

"You run away and you will never be free of her; you will just moon over her from farther afield. You need to accept that she failed you and find someone who will not."

"And what if it was I who failed her?"

"Nonsense! Her head was turned by flowery speeches, indulgence, and constant grand gifts; those are not the things to create a stable, strong marriage."

"I could never utter the words her husband does," Richard said with a shudder.

"Anyone who needs that type of flummery is not the one for you. When you accept that, you will see you had a lucky escape. I am hoping this gathering will prove to you that there are girls out there who will appreciate you. I have chosen carefully."

"Yet you have invited wallflowers, all of whom are around my own age. That is hardly going to guarantee my having an heir, plus you say you want great-nieces and great-nephews. Little chance of that if I marry a barren spinster."

"It is when you utter such poppycock that I am reminded you are the spawn of my stupid brother. I would expect him to come out with such heartless nonsense. You are above such comments."

Richard glowered at his aunt. "And with those words, I curse you to the devil for the comparison."

"Stop behaving like him and be true to yourself; you are far nicer when you stop acting the cad."

Richard moved to the fireplace, throwing on some coals and staring into the fire as the flames started to wrap themselves around the new fuel. He faced his aunt when the fire had taken hold once more, brushing his hands of any coal dust. She had not stopped watching him as he pondered, but had remained silent; she was more than aware that he hated any suggestion that he was like his father. When he turned towards her, any sign of annoyance had gone, to be replaced with a look of uncertainty that made him seem far younger than his six and twenty years.

"What if I am like him? How can I marry and bring children into the world if there is the slightest chance I would treat them in the way I was, even if I do manage to forget Bea and wed? I would not wish that future on my worst enemy, let alone my own offspring." He no longer sounded the disdainful nonesuch that many of his friends considered him. This was the real Richard, the one filled with doubt and misgivings that he kept well hidden from the wider world.

Marie stood and walked across the room to him. Reaching up and putting her hands on his cheeks, she forced him to look at her. "You are not him, or I would not be here now. As much as he was my own brother, I could only abide being near him because of you, and even then only for short periods. If I detected any of his characteristics in you, I would have banished you from my home long ago. You may utter the odd sentence that is reminiscent of him, but that is all."

"Sometimes I hear myself speak, and it is as if he is in my head. I am the master of the put-downs because I learned from the best."

"You could have become one of the best of the *ton* if you had shown your real nature. Instead, because of your father, and then more so with your broken engagement, you chose to become this odd version of yourself, never letting anyone close enough to see what you are really like."

"I will never let anyone treat me as they did. I refuse to be at anyone's mercy ever again," Richard said quietly. "If that means I wear a mask for most of the time, so be it."

"You are a better man than he could ever be, and you need to break the spell that binds you to Bea. She is not and never was the one for you. It is important to me to see you content to make up for the years after your mother died, which is why I need you happily settled before I breathe my last."

"You will be around for years yet."

"I hope so, but I want to see you with someone who brings out the best in you."

"And how will that happen?"

"Be yourself; stop this acting nonsense."

"You make it sound so easy."

"It is, and do not worry about the wallflowers; I did not invite them with you in mind. I have also invited Claude; it is time he settled down too."

Richard burst into laughter, no longer melancholy. "Do they know what awaits them? The poor devils."

"Not only is it time you were married, but Claude also needs a wife. I cannot spend the remainder of my days rescuing him from every scrape he gets himself into."

"As I have also had to play the rescuer a time or two, I cannot fault your sentiments, but will a wife really tame him? And will he consider a wallflower? You know what he is like. He is more likely to want a wealthy young debutante."

"If he wishes to continue receiving an allowance from me, he will do as I bid. I do think he was swapped at birth. I still cannot accept that he is my son, though he resembles my husband, God rest his soul, more than I care to admit, which means I cannot disown him for not being mine," Marie said with resignation.

"Aunt, you are wicked."

"No, I am not. Just realistic. There is no point pretending that my son is anything but a wastrel and a numbskull."

"Yet you are going to encourage him to marry some poor chit. That is not a nice thing to do to anyone, let alone some unsuspecting spinster."

"Fortunately, there are girls out there who would overlook his faults to receive the large inheritance I am to leave to her."

"But if she marries, Claude will have full control of their finances. It would take him six months to go through any inheritance he has access to, and then there would be two of them in the suds instead of just one."

"I will convince him that I am giving his wife a portion of his inheritance, and he will not be able to touch it."

Richard frowned at his aunt's words. "That is not very fair to the girl. He will try to browbeat her into handing over the money. Have you forgotten how he can go on for days on end without stopping his incessant whining? For I have not. I am sure my ears ache afterwards. A wife could not stand up to him as we do. Thankfully, he is in awe of you, but you will not always be there to protect her."

"Do not worry, I have not chosen a sacrificial lamb. The woman I have heard about is more than capable of standing up to him and able to hold her own when faced with his worst side, but in case I am wrong, there are others who might be suitable. I am sure one of the chits I have invited will be strong enough to withstand a life with Claude."

"I hope you are right or I will have something to say on the matter, for I cannot stand by and let a wrong be committed, even by you," Richard said firmly. "At least with Claude here, the pressure will be off my marrying; you will be too busy soothing the ruffled feathers he has caused. It might turn out to be an amusing house party after all."

"Please be open to the possibility of something long-lasting with one of the women I have invited. I have been shocking and invited more ladies than gentlemen, which will no doubt be commented on. If you do not marry at the end, I will know that I have done my best, and I hope you will have enjoyed yourself; that is all I can ask."

"That is an easy promise to give. A houseful of pretty girls is not really a hardship. I am just not giving you any promises that I will marry one of them."

"Just accept that I have to try. If I fail, then I can do no more meddling. For once, I will stop scheming. Reluctantly, because it will mean that you will continue to hanker after something that was not real."

"I cannot understand your train of thought. Of course what I had with Bea was real; I was engaged to her, for goodness' sake."

"She was never truly committed to you; anyone could see that. I pointed it out and got my nose snapped off for my pains, but it turned out I was right."

Richard refused to be dragged into going over the time he and his aunt had almost fallen out irrevocably. "As long as we are clear about the fact that I will be as single as I am now at the end of these two weeks, I can accept your attempt at meddling. In truth, all bluster aside, I cannot imagine ever finding a woman who would interest me above a sennight, let alone the rest of my days." The words *apart from Bea* were left unsaid, but they both knew that he had thought them.

"There is someone out there who will attract you. If your father could find a decent woman who could put up with his unreasonableness, I am sure you can find a woman who adores you."

"I think that is a compliment, but I am not quite sure." Richard shook his head at his aunt.

"If you did not resemble your mother so much, I would definitely claim you as my own." Marie smiled at him. "You are more like me in personality and outlook than any other family member I have ever come across."

"I suppose it means I am to look forward to a crotchety old age in which I am a menace to those younger than me and manage everyone's lives, whether they like it or not." Richard stepped away from her so he was out of striking distance.

"I think I will leave you as Claude's guardian."

"He is three and thirty!" Richard laughed.

"He would believe it if it was in my will."

"I might have to murder you now, just in case you are being serious."

"That would certainly make the house party interesting."

Chapter Two

"I wish Sophia and Caroline were accompanying us," Isabelle Carrington said as the carriage sped through the Hampshire countryside. "I do not like it when we are not all together."

"You will just have to be happy being a three instead of a five," Amelia Beckett consoled. "You should be careful, or you will have Patricia and me thinking you are unhappy with our company."

"And I might spend the whole week crying at the insult," Patricia Leaver said to her friend, trying to maintain a serious expression.

"Oh, pfft, you know what I mean. It is good fun when we are all together. I hate it when any of us are apart."

"Only because there are fewer people to talk to on the wallflower benches," Amelia teased.

"I suppose it will be different seating, but the same result at this party. I have wondered why we were invited," Isabelle mused.

"Marie Greenwood is a good friend of mine," Mrs. Enid Leaver, Patricia's grandmother, said. "She's the earl's aunt and tells me that she wants to see both her son and the earl married. She is clearly not viewing any of you as wallflowers or she would not have invited you. Marie is a shrewd woman and would never invite anyone she did not think worthy of joining her family."

"I ask again, why have we been invited?" Isabelle said, but she laughed when saying the words. "I have seen the Earl of Douglas, and he is gorgeous. Perhaps I will secure myself a husband after all, if his aunt is determined to see him married. There are definitely worse husbands to have."

Amelia frowned. "I do not think I have ever seen him."

"He does not come out in society too much, but he is noticed wherever he goes. He has dark hair and eyes but a remote nature, like some sort of gothic hero. You would remember him, I am sure," Isabelle said.

"You really should be writing books or poetry with your way with words," Amelia teased.

"Especially when she is being far too generous," Patricia said.

"Oh, really? Please tell me he looks like a gargoyle!" Amelia appealed.

Laughing at Isabelle's shocked expression, Patricia shook her head. "I am sorry to disappoint you. He is very attractive, but he spends most of his time looking down on everyone through his very superior quizzing glass." Mimicking Richard, she made the others smile.

"Sounds just like the type of man we should avoid, although I doubt he will look in our direction," Amelia said.

Isabelle grimaced. "Which cannot be said for the owner's son."

"Mr. Greenwood," Patricia groaned.

"Oh no!" Amelia exclaimed. "No wonder you told me very little of this house party before we set out," she said. "If I knew he was to be there, my agreement to the scheme might not have been so forthcoming."

"You would leave us to fend for ourselves?" Patricia asked, all mock indignation.

"Perhaps not, but he gives me the creeps when he is just looking at someone. I would hate to dance with him, and that from a woman who sits on the wallflower benches and is usually grateful for any dance!"

"Exactly!" Isabelle agreed. "We have to make a pact that we are never alone when Mr. Greenwood is around."

"Oh, most certainly." Amelia shuddered. "I pity anyone he sets his attention on."

"He does take a little getting used to," Enid said. "But he is a wealthy man in his own right and will become more so when he inherits after Marie has died, though I hope that will not be for years to come."

"Grandmamma, you would see one of us married to him? *Me?*" Patricia exclaimed.

"Of course not, and Marie will be fully aware of that; she has always been honest about his failings. I am hopeful that the earl is looking to marry, and as he is about your age, it would be perfect for one of you to secure him. I know Marie thinks very highly of him, more than her son, if she were being honest."

"You are hoping one of us will secure him?" Patricia asked.

"Why would I not? Marie does not suffer fools and always speaks with fondness."

"He is an earl; the title alone gives him the right to be spoken well of," Amelia said.

"Not in Marie's case. It would not matter if he was a duke, she would be honest in her opinions. You should hear what she says about her son; she is positively caustic."

"She sounds an interesting character," Amelia said.

"She sounds terrifying," Isabelle said.

"She is both." Enid smiled at the girls. "But she likes spirit in a person; I am sure she will approve of you three."

As they turned into the grounds of Greenwood House, they eagerly looked out of the window as the carriage trundled down the driveway. As the trees parted to reveal the turning circle in front of the red brick house, Amelia smiled at her friends.

"One thing is for certain, we are going to be living in comfort these next two weeks if the outside is anything to go by."

As they entered the large square hallway, there was a hive of activity. Amelia looked around, appreciating the black and white marble floor, the cream marble fireplace, and the vases and statues carefully placed around the entrance hall to enhance the overall look of the space.

"This is a beautiful house," she said as she handed bonnet, gloves, and shawl to a footman.

"Thank you. I pride myself on having the best designers, and I cannot stand vulgarity or too much ostentation. I prefer the house to appear elegant rather than cluttered," Marie said, coming to greet her guests. "Enid, it is good to see you again. I am glad you could make it."

"I would not miss a chance to watch your machinations for anything," Enid replied as she embraced her friend.

"Beast," Marie laughed.

"You remember Patricia," Enid said to Marie.

"I do. You are the double of your mother; she would have been thrilled to know you look so much like her," Marie said, turning to Patricia.

"Mrs. Greenwood." Patricia curtsied. "Please allow me to introduce my friends, Miss Isabelle Carrington and Miss Amelia Beckett."

"I hope the rest of you have as good taste as Miss Beckett," Marie said with a nod towards Amelia.

"I love building design, inside and out, which I know does not make me sound the best dinner partner to have, but I assure you that I will not bore your guests to death," Amelia said.

Marie smiled. "Glad to hear it. Come, now, let me send you with my housekeeper to settle into your rooms, and then I can introduce you to the others in the party who have arrived."

After refreshing themselves and changing out of their travel-weary clothes, the three met Enid on the stairs before going down to the drawing room.

"I am happy that we three are sharing a room," Patricia said as they descended the oak staircase. "I feel less intimidated when we are together as one."

Amelia tsked. "Patricia, one day you will come to appreciate your true value. None of us is any less worthy than any of the other guests here; plus, we have the protection of your grandmother, who is capable of intimidating anyone she chooses."

"That I am," Enid agreed.

"We do not have the fortunes or the young age needed to recommend us," Patricia defended.

"No, but we are not paupers either. I refuse to beg forgiveness for not being quite rich or attractive enough to be acceptable to the elite of the *ton*," Amelia said. "If that is all they are looking for when seeking a wife, then I am happy to be a spinster." She was not being totally honest with her friends, which they were fully aware. There was another reason she never wanted to marry, but that was known by only those closest to her, and out of respect, was never mentioned or acknowledged.

"You should not speak like that. After all, you could fall in love with Lord Douglas," Isabelle teased.

"I very much doubt it from your description of him," Amelia said. "I would end up knocking his quizzing glass out of his hand if he constantly glared at me through it. What an especially annoying habit to have, and how condescending."

"I could see you stamping on it, just to make sure he could not use it again," Patricia said.

"If a job is worth doing, it is worth doing well," Amelia said loftily, a laugh in her voice.

The three were announced into the drawing room, their amusement lighting up their faces and giving their eyes an extra sparkle, such that the few men already within the room were more than willing to make their acquaintance, whether they were wallflowers or not.

WHEN THE DOOR to the drawing room closed, Richard and his valet stepped out of the doorway they had been standing in unnoticed. They had been coming out of the library when, on hearing the voices, they had held back.

Looking at his valet with raised eyebrows, Richard broke the silence between them. "It seems that whoever coined the saying 'you hear nothing good through eavesdropping' was speaking the truth."

"It is just the talk of silly young girls," the valet said.

"They did not sound silly or young," Richard said. "At least I do not need to trouble myself in being pleasant towards them."

"You promised your aunt," the valet cautioned, knowing exactly what Marie had said because Richard had repeated most of their conversation to him.

"Sam, you know as well as I that I only promised to be open to possibilities, nothing more. As I cannot risk having my quizzing glass smacked out of my hand regularly, I can immediately dismiss those three ladies." Richard was not overly offended by the comments. If he allowed himself to consider the context in which they were said, he would be slightly amused, but hearing them had stung a little, and the teasing note of the comments had not been fully appreciated by one who inwardly considered himself worthless in many respects. "I will enjoy giving them one of my set-downs."

Sam groaned, but chose to remain silent. When the devil took his master's mood, it was better to let him be until he returned to his old self. He would consider it the occasional time when the ghost of the old master influenced his master. It was not often, but it was upsetting when it did, for the young lord had suffered enough if the nightmares were anything to go by.

Richard entered the drawing room, quizzing glass firmly in place, taking the opportunity to pause and view the occupants gathered. The room was as grand and exquisitely laid out as the rest of his aunt's home, a marble fireplace taking pride of place in the main wall. Four large floor-to-ceiling windows overlooked a sprawling lawned area. The furniture was all high quality, but each piece was there because it was of use, not purely for decoration. On this occasion, the delights of the room were not what took Richard's attention. He scanned the group of those who were overtly looking at him or those more surreptitiously glancing his way. He wondered who his aunt had considered a suitable bride for him, for just as she had chosen one specifically for Claude, she would have done the same for him, just not admitted it for fear of frightening him off.

There were six mamas with their husbands and daughters who all seemed to be just out of the school room, which had Richard struggling to hold back a grimace. His aunt did not know him at all if she thought he would marry a chit who was barely more than a child; he would feel positively ancient next to them.

An additional two young ladies seemed to be together with a lone woman, who stood next to three gentlemen, one of whom was his cousin, Claude. Wonderful, Claude had brought two of his friends; the stay got better and better. Richard inwardly cursed. Finally, there were the wallflowers, unmistakable as they were set a little apart, who stood more confidently than the younger women in the room and barely glanced his way, as if accepting already that they were there to make numbers up. Though with this party, at least, this was not the case. He wondered if his aunt's friend was in on the scheme to marry one of them to Claude, as she stood with the wallflowers.

If he had been worried that they would try to ingratiate themselves to him, he no longer had that concern. He had clearly not been the attractive temptation that had drawn them to the house party, which was an unusual occurrence, for he was accustomed to being fawned over if there was a single woman looking for a husband.

His cousin diverted Richard's attention away from the wallflowers;

Claude was loud, dressed a little like the Regent in that he wore gaudy, bright clothes that struggled to stretch across his ample stomach. His tailors might hint that he needed a larger size, but Claude would scoff that they did not know their trade and demand they make his clothing to his usual size. As the years went by, the cloth was being stretched further than it was supposed to, and it distorted the patterns, making them into grotesque shapes, doing nothing for the look Claude considered he achieved when dressed in his finery. Richard sighed; he had never been close to his cousin, though they had lived under the same roof for a number of years. Even when Richard was fully engrossed in his public persona, he could find little in common with Claude.

Nodding to his aunt, he followed her to be introduced to everyone gathered, quizzing glass tucked away for the moment. His attention kept drifting to the wallflowers as he moved around the room. As he looked at them, he wondered which was the one who objected to his quizzing glass. Was it the petite blonde with the blue eyes and glasses? Not if the way she blushed when one of the others whispered something to her was any indication. It could be the taller of the three, who had dull brown hair and brown eyes. She seemed very comfortable and nodded to his aunt and smiled as their eyes met briefly. He guessed she was the granddaughter of his aunt's friend; there was a similarity between them.

The last wallflower had her back to him; all he could see was her rich auburn hair, highlighted by cream flowers. Her figure was slender and elegant, though not tall; Richard just knew that this was the one. She was clearly not interested that he had entered the room; instead, she was entertaining her friends. He was tempted to put her in her place as soon as he had the opportunity, not a magnanimous thought, but he could not acknowledge to himself that she had upset him with her comments.

Being introduced to everyone reinforced that staying with his aunt was a mistake. It was clear most of the young women were there to try to secure him, a pity for Claude, but it was not vanity that drove Richard to the conclusion. Claude very often had shown himself at a disadvantage when in company, being self-indulgent, entitled, and loud. Richard had tried to help Claude over the years, but because of Richard's unhappy childhood and inner vulnerability, Claude had always considered himself superior and had never listened to the hints or advice Richard had offered.

"Happy to see you, cousin," Claude boomed out. "Come to see what scraps I leave for you?"

Richard cringed at the vulgarity of the statement said so openly. "I have come to spend a few weeks with my aunt," he replied, tone cold as ice.

"Always was a bore," Claude said to his friends. "I intend enjoying myself to the full, and who can blame me when surrounded by so many pretty fillies?" Claude raised his glass to the people who were now looking at him warily. It was clear some of the party had not met him prior to their invitation. They were probably regretting their decision to attend, whether it was coming to the end of the Season or not.

Richard glared at his cousin. "You will give your mother the courtesy of acting like a well-mannered human being whilst she has guests," he hissed.

"And when did you become the agent of my mother?" Claude snapped back.

"From the moment I noticed you were little more than a coxcomb," Marie said. "Albeit a rich one."

Claude glowered at his mother. "One who cannot access all his funds, so it does not matter how rich I am."

"Yes, and do not think when I die anything will change, for your cousin will have control of your fortune then, and there are strict instructions to be less lenient than I was," Marie said.

"I am of age, Mother!" Claude hissed at Marie, not wishing the others to overhear the conversation. But everyone could hear, for he could not speak quietly, especially when agitated, though the visitors tried to pretend not to be listening.

"When you start acting like a grown-up, you will be treated as such. Come, Richard, I want to introduce you to the granddaughter of a good friend of mine," Marie said, completely ignoring that her son was seething with rage.

"You should be more circumspect if you wish to see him married. He needs to appear in a good light," Richard said quietly as they approached the wallflowers.

"I want the one who marries him to have no doubt about what or who she will be taking on, for she needs to be strong," Marie replied.

"Then why invite so many so young?" Richard asked.

"To fool Claude into thinking he has a choice, and hopefully to tempt you, of course."

Richard suddenly felt pity for the wallflowers; it was clear his aunt had indeed chosen one of them to persuade into marrying Claude. As they turned at his approach, he reached for his quizzing glass, but stopped when his hand was on his waistcoat pocket. He had looked at the one with the auburn hair as she turned and had been struck with the most compelling storm-gray eyes he had ever seen. Wallflowers were supposed to be plain, were they not? Yet, he was taken aback by her, not by her beauty, for she could not be considered as such; though she was no ape-leader, more handsome, with a confidence and grace that surrounded her. This was not the wilting, snide spinster he had expected to see, and he felt the urge, no, the need, to know her better. Completely disconcerted by such a visceral reaction to a stranger, it made him falter.

Richard noticed her eyes following the movement of his hand towards his pocket, and she looked as if she was about to burst out laughing. The uncertainty he usually hid behind his cold, aloof exterior was ignited at her expression, and it was probably because no one had ever looked so unconcerned about being introduced to him, never mind had the gall to laugh at him.

Her reaction towards him made his response to her even more confusing. It was not arrogance on his part to have expected some sort of deference when he faced her, it was what everyone did, but it was the first time he had wished it to happen. Dropping his hand to his side, he could feel the heat of embarrassment creep up his neck, but he would not show outwardly that he was out of sorts.

Marie conducted the introductions, and everyone bowed and curt-sied, but Richard could hardly take his eyes off Amelia. Her amusement had turned to a look of curiosity; he would not classify it as interest, but as if she was wondering what he would do next. And was there a little disappointment in her expression, indicating that he had not acted in the way she had wished him to? He hoped he had surprised her, because she had certainly affected him.

"I think I know your elder brother, Miss Beckett," he said, trying to gain control of the situation, his voice a little more choked than normal.

"Oh really? Were you one of the crowd who was sent home to rusticate in the last term you attended at Oxford?" Amelia asked.

"No, although I heard of the events leading up to the action which caused his expulsion, I was very much on the outside of their group."

"Ah, I was hoping you would be able to shed some light on what really happened with the flagpole, for Father has forbidden Jacob to speak about it to anyone and, for once, my brother is doing as he was bid, mostly."

"Mostly?" Richard asked.

"Jacob is very proud of what they did and cannot help himself in revealing some of the details. It almost makes it worse, knowing only part of the story, but he knows Father will be angry with him if he glories too much in his wrongdoings."

The incident in question was that of hanging the undergarments of one of the master's wives on the flagpole. It had outraged many and been hailed as genius by others. It was the type of prank he would expect to shock most young ladies. Richard's expression must have revealed some of his inner surprise that she was so open with her knowledge of such an act, as her eyes lit up once more in amusement.

"I beg pardon if my words have shocked you, my lord." She smiled sweetly, clearly not meaning a single word she said.

"Not at all. I am just surprised your brother is not more circumspect around you, that is all." Richard's tone was every bit the disapproving elder, though there was little difference in age between them.

"He is sometimes," Amelia said, at which Patricia let out a coughed laugh. "Fine. He is completely outrageous and revels in the storytelling of his exploits afterwards."

"I will have to seek your brother out next time I am in London; he sounds as if he would brighten any dull evening," Marie said.

"Oh, he does."

"Come, Richard, let us re-join the Misses Jones. They are particular favorites of mine," Marie said with a nod and a smile at the wallflowers.

Richard followed his aunt, wishing he could have shown more of his displeasure to Amelia. That would have shown her that she should be more guarded in how she spoke to strangers. That was the thought that he muttered to himself as he crossed the drawing room, but at the same time, he felt compelled and intrigued by her. No one he had ever met before would have dared to mention such a risqué practical joke on first meeting. He wondered if she had set out to purposely shock him, but then acknowledged that he was the one who had mentioned her brother, not her. He was disturbed from his confusing musings by his aunt.

"What do you think of her?" Marie asked.

"Who?" He panicked that his aunt had noticed his reaction towards Amelia.

"Miss Beckett, of course," Marie answered. "She is the perfect one for Claude, I am sure of it. She is strong-willed, intelligent, and not afraid to speak her mind or stand up for herself. I have been considering her as a perfect match since Enid first mentioned her."

Richard stopped in his tracks. "Tell me you are funning with me?"

"Why on earth would I do that?"

"She is not the one for Claude. She would never accept your proposal." Why did his statements feel like he was trying to convince himself as much as his aunt? He had only just met the woman, and she had done nothing to endear herself to him, yet the thought of her being attached to Claude made his stomach roil.

"Everyone has a price. The family needs funds, and there are two younger sisters who, along with herself, have virtually no dowry to speak of; she will come to see the advantage of the match. After all, there are no other suitors competing for her hand," Marie said in such a cold, matter-of-fact way that Richard was reminded that his aunt was a blood relation to his father.

"Aunt, you are wrong in this instance. You cannot condemn her to what a life with Claude will be."

Marie narrowed her eyes at her nephew. "Has she turned your head?"

"No! Of course not."

"Good. There is a spark about her that is appealing, and that is what will help her with Claude, but she would be no good for you. She would challenge you, and although initially, you might find it entertaining, you would hate it and her eventually. Bea was too much of a flibbertigibbet and flighty to match, but you need a compliant wife. Trust me on this, I have thought about every aspect you both need in wives. Now come and talk to the Misses Jones."

For the first time in his life, he knew his aunt was very wrong in her assumptions, and the feeling of dread in his stomach was something that would not be easily moved. He tried to put it down to the fact that she was trying to match him to a schoolroom chit, but it was the thought that Amelia might indeed have the need to accept the offer his aunt was going to make to her. Trying to dampen down the panic that threatened to make him demand that his aunt change her plans, he could not utter a word because he knew her too well. Once she had made her mind up about something, there was no persuading her otherwise.

He would have to put aside his unique and somewhat disturbing response to Amelia and put it down to the fact that it was refreshing that she had not been like the others who had been introduced to him. There was nothing more to it than that.

When Amelia laughed at something one of her friends said, his stomach tightened. Why did he have the overwhelming urge to spoil his aunt's plans? She could not marry Claude; he would ruin her spirit. That the same spirit had offended him only half an hour previously was irrelevant. Questioning his motives, he decided that he was purely looking out for a lamb going to the slaughter, that was all; there were no other feelings involved on his part.

He almost laughed at how unconvincing he sounded to himself.

Chapter Three

THANKFULLY FOR AMELIA'S happiness, she had no idea of the plans that Marie had in store for her and enjoyed her first evening with everyone. Marie was not so obvious to have sat Amelia next to Claude during dinner, so although there was not an even split of gentlemen and ladies, it was an entertaining evening. Amelia had gone to bed and had an untroubled night's sleep, rising fresh in the morning, completely unaware her future was being planned.

As the early risers gathered around the breakfast table, a ride out was arranged for later in the morning, but Amelia declined to go. The youngest of the Misses Evans had taken to doing anything that she could to promote herself and took the opportunity to undermine Amelia when she said that she would not be joining the riding party.

"It is such a beautiful morning, and the area is fine. Do you not wish to explore?" Sarah asked.

"I would like to explore, but not on horseback," Amelia said, tucking into eggs and thick slices of ham.

"Do you not have a horse of your own? We brought ours with us, but I am sure Mrs. Greenwood has one you could borrow."

Amelia smiled. "I do not have my own, purely because unless I am seated in a carriage, I have no wish to travel by horse."

The eldest Miss Evans leaned over, speaking in a stage whisper. "If you are a poor rider, then I applaud your hesitance; none of us would wish to appear at a disadvantage to the earl when there are so many vying for his attention." That Richard was also at the table did not seem to be an indication that she should be more circumspect.

"Miss Beckett is a perfectly good horsewoman," Patricia said tartly.

"Then why would she not take the opportunity to show off her prowess?" Miss Evans asked with genuine bafflement.

Amelia sighed; she did not wish to air her reasoning to strangers, but she also knew that she had to stop this subject, especially as it was obvious that Richard could hear every word. She did not know which was worse, the fact he would consider her poor, or that he would find out that she was damaged. Not knowing why he thinking ill of her was so disturbing, for she could never be considered vain, she concluded that it would be another reason he could look at her with that disdainful expression of his.

"I was bitten badly by a horse a few years ago. It was a long and painful road to recovery, and I still have the scars to remind me of my foolishness every day. I do not wish to go through that experience again, so I am happiest when surrounded by some form of carriage rather than be so close as to be seated on the animal."

"Oh, so you are maimed?" Sarah asked. Amelia hoped the words were said with pity and not the glee that seemed to be in Sarah's tone of voice. "I understand now why you are so afraid."

"I would not say that I am afraid, just intent on self-preservation, and no wish to repeat the recovery I went through," Amelia said.

"I am sure the mothers would enjoy your company, for you must be nearer their age than ours," Sarah said with a sidelong glance at Richard.

Amelia could not help the laugh that escaped her. "I am sure I am," she said. Isabelle and Patricia looked annoyed at the obvious set-down, but Amelia was not concerned about it at all.

She noticed that Richard was frowning at no one in particular and wondered who it was directed at. It was probably that he was of the opinion that he was in the presence of someone who was far from perfect and was disgusted that the company was not the finest society had to offer. She was being harsh on him and she knew it, but the conversation and Richard's now glowering expression were reminders of how she would repel any man as soon as they knew the truth about her state. It was the reason she had accepted that she was to remain a spinster. She saw the reality of her scars in the looking glass; she could only imagine what a man's reaction would be on their wedding night if she were ever to agree to a marriage.

She was not one to dwell on self-pity and focused her thoughts on Richard's propensity to frown so much, for his features were handsome. In fact, he was striking; raven-black hair and ice-blue eyes certainly made him stand out, but apart from being attractive, there was something in his eyes which hinted at there being more about him than his stern persona. It stirred her curiosity and something else; she was compelled to know what was behind the façade, for though she had only just met him, she was convinced that he was not all that he portrayed, almost as if her own troubled soul had detected another.

The party split up after they had their fill of breakfast, and Amelia enjoyed a walk around the gardens. It was clear that Marie also employed the best gardeners because the grounds were as exquisite as the house. Each area was carefully laid out, with planting designed to complement the features, statues, and grottos in perfect harmony.

After spending an enjoyable hour exploring, and a quite ridiculous amount of time thinking about the earl, she turned back towards the house. Passing the sunken garden, which was close to the building, she noticed the position of a bench overlooking one of the wings of the house. It was too much of a temptation for her to resist, and so she sat, taking out her drawing pad. Starting to draw the building, she took care to include every tiny detail. Only when she had sat for some time, engrossed in her task, did she become aware of a conversation taking place through an open window behind her. Claude's voice rang out loud and clear, which surprised her as she had presumed he had joined the riding party.

"I will not have this interference in my life!" Claude shouted. Amelia could not see him behind the voile curtain blowing in the open window, but she could hear him as if he was standing next to her.

"You will do as I bid. After all, I am arranging everything with your best interests at heart, you absolute fool." Marie sounded angrier than her son.

"And I am supposed to be grateful that you wish me to marry a dried-up spinster?" Claude demanded. "Do you want the line to die out?"

"When faced with you, I sometimes feel it would be a good thing."

Amelia had been putting her book and pencils away in order to put some distance between herself and the argument, but on hearing those words, it stopped her in her tracks. They could only be talking about one of her group if referring to a spinster. The other women were far too young to be classed as such. Stiffening with indignation, she remained seated, refusing to leave until she had heard more.

"You are keeping my inheritance from me." Claude was clearly pacing, as his voice came and went as he moved. "I will challenge you."

"And how will you find the funds to do that? What will happen the next time you exceed your allowance and debts need paying off?" Marie taunted.

"If I had my dues, there would be no need for me to beg, but you enjoy being the one in charge, so you can lord it over me."

"You fool! I am ensuring that we are not both destitute! Two thousand a year should be more than enough when you have no other responsibilities than your own pleasure to think about, but no, you cannot help but waste money. You will marry, and your wife will take over what I have started."

"There are other ways of taking what is mine," Claude said.

"Are you threatening me, boy?"

"Good God, no! Do you think me capable of that?" Amelia could hear the genuine horror in Claude's voice and had to give him credit for being as shocked as she was at Marie's words.

"With you, Claude, nothing would surprise me," Marie responded, sounding older and more defeated than she normally did.

"Killing my only remaining parent is not my style, Mother, as much as I despise you at the moment, so sleep easily. I can promise that I will be taking what is mine, though, so you had better accept that."

"You are talking in riddles, but know this, you will be announcing your engagement at the end of this house party."

Claude snorted. "Only if I can try the delights of her flesh first. Whilst I am forced to remain at this damned party, I might as well have an enjoyable time. If you are in cahoots with her, you had better warn her to prepare herself, for I will not be leg-shackled to someone who does not stir me."

"You are disgusting."

"Consider it as my response to your being so damned controlling. At least you cannot stop me from doing as I wish in that regard."

Amelia had heard enough. She felt sick to the stomach and hurried inside before either of them moved from the room. Quickly making her way to the drawing room, she joined the mothers who had gathered there. She did not wish to be anywhere alone. When her friends had agreed to stick together to avoid Claude before they had reached the house, it had been said with some seriousness but no real evidence that they would need to be so careful, but now there was a real chance that one of them was in danger of being ruined by Claude. They were suddenly in a very precarious situation.

Annoyed at the high-handed way Marie was going about her plan to determine who was to marry Claude, Amelia tried to concentrate on the conversations going on around her, but thankfully, the women still considered her as competition for the prize of marrying the earl and did not engage with her. She could have smiled when registering that none of them ever mentioned Claude as a possible husband for their daughters, and after what she had heard, she could not blame them one bit.

When the riding group returned and she had joined Isabelle and Patricia in their chamber, telling them what she had overheard, they were both as horrified as she had been.

"Why would she choose one of us?" Isabelle asked in disbelief.

"She must think we have the strength of character to keep her son under some sort of control," Amelia said, correctly guessing Marie's motivation.

"It must be me," Patricia said. "I say this with no wish to be the one chosen, but she did not know either of you before this party. How could she repay my grandmother's friendship by wishing me to marry *him*?"

"None of us will be marrying him," Amelia said. "I refuse to let us be a sacrifice just because he has been overindulged and is now a spoiled, offensive man. I could hardly believe when she said that he has two thousand a year and still manages to have debts."

"It is such a lot of money," Patricia said.

"Is it a temptation?" Amelia asked, smiling.

"No!" Patricia choked back a groan. "I am happy to never marry if my only option is Mr. Greenwood, however much money he has."

"We should leave before there is the opportunity for her to put whatever plan she has concocted into action. She might contrive a compromising situation if he refuses to comply with her wishes," Isabelle said.

"From what he said, we are more at risk from him doing the compromising and then abandoning us, though I would rather be cast out than forced into a marriage to him," Isabelle said. "We should leave."

"And upset one of the most feared matrons of society by snubbing her and leaving her house party early? Not a chance!" Patricia said.

"Who we did not know until this weekend," Isabelle pointed out.

"She named you on the invitation, so you might not have known her, but she was aware of you."

"Oh dear, she would really make our lives hell, wouldn't she?"

"Yes." Patricia had known Marie the longest and knew without doubt there would be consequences if they caused a fuss and left.

"We will stay unless it gets too uncomfortable. I think there is some merit in what Patricia says, but I am not about to put up with anything to avoid upsetting our hostess," Amelia started. "We must be very careful about staying together. His words made my skin crawl."

"Agreed," Patricia said. "And if it does get too uncomfortable here, I would be willing to go home."

"Do you think your grandmother knows about Mrs. Greenwood's scheme?"

"I hope not," Patricia said. "I can ask."

"Do not mention anything for now, for if Mrs. Greenwood finds out that we are aware of her plans, we do not know how she will react. We can use the knowledge we have to our advantage, for now at least."

"I will not be pleased if Grandmamma does know about this and has not thought to tell us," Patricia said.

"You will not be the only one," Amelia ground out.

AMELIA SWALLOWED A groan to see that she was to be seated next to Claude for their evening meal, although it gave her a little satisfaction to see that Claude looked as disgusted with the arrangement as she did.

What she did not know was that Richard had seen who the seat next to Claude was assigned to and had contrived to rearrange things a little. After what his aunt had revealed, he was not able in all good conscience to leave her to Claude's mercy. He refused to acknowledge that he wished to speak to her for his own satisfaction. Ignoring the glare that Marie sent him as his seated himself next to Amelia, he turned away from his aunt.

"Good evening, Miss Beckett."

"Good evening, my lord. Did you enjoy your trip out today?" Amelia asked, trying to ignore that Richard somehow felt larger when close to her. She had felt his leg brush against hers as he sat, causing every nerve ending to come alive, and feeling as if the space between them was not enough, yet she did not wish to move away. His being so near sent a rush of warmth through her, which was both a surprise and an annoyance. She reminded herself that she could not allow herself any fanciful notions of being attracted to someone. For the first time since her accident, the thought of never experiencing the love of a man saddened her.

She might have teased him on their first interaction, but she was closer to him now, and he seemed more handsome than ever. It was no wonder he was chased by many; even without his title, he would have been coveted as a desirable husband. The thought of him marrying had her feeling bereft for some reason. She was usually so positive; it was strange that he made her long for something that could not be. Though when he looked at her, his eyes were still the cold ice blue of a lofty aristocrat, enabling her to compose herself and speak as if his presence had absolutely no effect on her.

"It was an opportunity to exercise my horse," Richard answered honestly. He had been harassed the whole ride by one or other of the young women; only Patricia and Isabelle had left him alone, which he had been exceedingly grateful for. It was not the done thing to speak across a guest, but Richard looked at Claude, who had turned in surprise to see Richard near his end of the table; his mother usually kept him close to her. "Why did you not join us? Afraid my prowess would put you to shame?"

"Pah, as if that would be an issue for me! That chestnut of yours is getting decidedly haggard. I do not know why you keep him; it does your reputation no good to be seen on such an elderly hack," Claude mocked.

"I do not discard things because they get old," Richard responded.

"How utterly gallant of you," Claude sneered.

"If my prowess was not the reason you did not join us, what was?" Richard persisted. He had noticed that his aunt was out of sorts since everyone had returned, but she had waved away his questioning when he had spoken to her.

"I had to speak to Mother, and she was being damned unreasonable," Claude snapped. "I will have things my way; just you watch me." With the last comment, he almost turned his back on them and started to speak to a Miss Simpson, who had been seated on his other side. She was young and pretty and seemed slightly in awe of Claude, but it was clear he was determined to charm her rather than be his usual obnoxious self, so Richard did not feel that his cousin would be outrageous, for now at least.

"I pride myself on being an observer of people, but even the most inattentive amongst us will have noticed that you have been well and truly dismissed, my lord," Amelia said quietly.

"I have, have I not?" Richard responded dryly. "Oh well, arguing with one's family is not *de rigueur* at the dining table."

"No."

He was surprised that she had not excused his *faux pas*. Most young women would allow him to get away with anything if it meant they looked to advantage because of it. He had the distinct impression she would never be one to fawn over him, and he liked the thought of having someone who would speak honestly to him. For some reason, the fact that she had been the one to make the comments about his habit of intimidation with his quizzing glass no longer angered him as it had. The pull of her was making him forget anything other than that he needed to know her better.

"Though it is entertaining to watch," Amelia continued.

"And what do you gain from watching people, Miss Beckett? I cannot say I am interested enough in society to do the same."

Amelia smiled. "It passes the time, and in some cases can offer amusement in what sometimes can be a very dreary evening."

"I shudder to think what dire invitations you receive if you consider your evenings so tedious that you are forced to watch those around you. I thought all young ladies enjoyed every ball and rout they attend."

"Perhaps if they are constantly dancing, yes, I can see that an evening would be thoroughly enjoyable, but when confined to the wallflower benches or sitting with the chaperones, one has to take one's amusements from the limited opportunities presented."

"Yet you attend the balls?" Richard was intrigued again. Why was this woman not married? Even the smell of jasmine that surrounded her was enticing; it was rich, fruity and sensual, a description Richard had never expected to make about perfume. "I would rather not go if I knew beforehand that the evening would be tedious," he continued, trying to keep the conversation from anything that could be misconstrued, though he had the overwhelming urge to touch her. He must be suffering from pity for the girl. That must be it, he tried to convince himself, for his thoughts and impulses were totally unexpected.

Amelia laughed, taking her time putting slices of roast beef on her plate. "And offend the hostesses of the *ton*? No, my lord. I might be considered more outspoken than perhaps I should be, but even I am not *that* foolish."

"Ah, so you do adhere to societal rules? I thought you were of a similar character to your brother from what you said when we first met," Richard said, eyebrows raised.

Pausing to put down the plate of beef and pick up a bowl of roasted potatoes, she looked at Richard in amusement. "Come, my lord.

We neither of us are in the first flush of youth; we know exactly how society works. I usually check my audience before uttering anything inappropriate, unlike my brother."

"Yet you were very quick to be open about him."

"You said that you knew him. I admit I presumed you knew him better than you actually do. On reflection, the two of you would definitely not get on well together."

Richard stiffened at her words. "And why is that?"

"I cannot imagine you getting into a scrape," Amelia said, looking at him as if assessing him. "No, your sense of propriety would not allow that, but I am willing to hear that I am mistaken."

"You seemed to quickly form an opinion."

"Perhaps, sometimes it is necessary." Amelia shrugged. "Are you not going to tell me that I am wrong? That you are as headstrong as my brother?"

"My exploits should not be spoken about in polite company." Richard was pleased to see the flicker of interest in her eyes and had the overwhelming urge to tell her some of the things he had been involved with, but as they usually involved gambling, drink, and married women in order to block his mind from thinking of Bea, he could not offer more.

"I am surprised and perhaps a little disbelieving." Amelia smiled at him in what he was quickly coming to know was her teasing expression. It was a look that suited her, lightening her eyes and making them sparkle.

"You seem to be the person here who I could never hope to impress. According to you, I am old and boring."

Amelia burst out laughing and placed her hand on his arm for a moment before recollecting herself and removing it, picking up her fork and hoping her flushed cheeks did not reveal the effect of touching him had on her. "Now do not take a pet, I beg of you! I did not say that you were boring, just that you were clearly not suited to belonging to the wilder of the friendship groups at Oxford. It is a compliment, I assure you."

"Hmmm, I see you have not excused the comment about my age." Richard had moved instinctively to place his hand over hers when she had touched him, and he fiddled with his glass to mask his movement. He could still feel the gentle weight of her hand on his arm, though she had removed it. The thought raced through his mind that she had branded him as hers, which was ridiculous. He was acting like someone smitten, and he was most certainly not. It was just a reaction to a handsome woman who was determined to fence verbally with him. He was responding because it was unusual and refreshing; there was no other reason.

"As I included my own age in that comment, it would be insincere to try and convince you that I meant anything other than what I said."

"At least I know where not to come when I am feeling low," Richard said dryly. "You could never be accused of pandering to the vanity of the higher ranks."

"I respect the rank, but the person needs to earn my good opinion." Amelia shrugged.

"I see." He was discomfited at every turn with this woman, but whereas he had wanted to be disdainful and give her a set-down for the comments he had overheard, he now wished to find out everything about her. No one could have been more surprised by the turn of events than him. Trying to get himself under control, he changed the subject to a safer one. "Did you enjoy your time in the garden?"

"I did. I enjoy company, but I also like some time alone. I was able to indulge my passion for drawing."

"Of what do you draw?"

Amelia grimaced. "I hate to admit it because it will not show me to any advantage, though it is probably too late for that already."

"Now I am very curious."

"I draw buildings," Amelia admitted.

"Really? Now that is not the reply I was expecting."

"Because young ladies are only allowed to draw flowers?"

Richard laughed. "No, but I admit I did presume that it would be landscapes."

Amelia wished he smiled and laughed more, but then decided that having those blue eyes warm with amusement could be dangerous for a woman who should know better. "I try not to broadcast my love of structures. I do not suppose I would have had such an interest except for being so restricted for so long."

"After your accident?"

"Or what could be classed as my foolishness," Amelia said. "The days recuperating were driving me to distraction, and when staring at the same view every day, I needed something to interest me."

"And you chose buildings?" Richard could not help the amusement in his voice and was gratified by the smile his words caused.

"I had limited options, but my father encouraged me and employed an architect to teach me the correct way to capture and create buildings."

"Create buildings? That goes beyond drawing as a hobby."

"It is just using my imagination, although I have designed a folly I would love to see built. And now I have the unenviable task of saying sorry to your aunt, for I promised I would not speak about buildings at the dinner table, and on one of my first meals here, I have done just that."

"I am glad you have."

"What? You did not expect me to speak of the price of muslin or the weather, or admit that I drew flowers and bowls of fruit?" Amelia teased.

"Please, no! To avoid those topics is a relief, believe me. Although my aunt will think our lively chatter is an indication that I am engaged in this farce of a party, it is mainly for my cousin."

Amelia wondered how much Richard knew of his aunt's plans, but gave him the benefit of the doubt. Being magnanimous towards him was easy with the compliment he had given her; she did not think that Richard had many lively conversations with strangers from what her friends had said. She did not wish to believe he would be involved in such a calculating scheme but could not understand why she wanted to think well of him on so little an acquaintance. "I take it we are not to have the pleasure of celebrating your engagement at the end of the party?"

"Good God, no!" Richard exclaimed.

Laughing at the words said with such feeling, Amelia could not help but tease him. "I could be offended at those words, but as I came with no expectations other than to enjoy myself, I will forgive you."

"I beg pardon. I meant no insult," Richard said stiffly, comprehending with some mortification how unintentionally gauche he had been. He was mortified, partly because he was never so revealing, but mainly because the blasted woman constantly unsettled him.

"And you gave none. It just means we can relax in each other's company without there being any danger of misunderstandings developing. It is tiresome when one offers friendship and it is misconstrued. After all, not every man is the catch he thinks he is," Amelia said, reaching for a plate of lamb cutlets. Amelia could see that Richard was taken aback by her words, but she smiled at him. "Do you not believe what I say?"

"I do, and that is what surprises me the most," Richard answered candidly. He had set out to give her a set-down, then he had felt he should be the one to rescue her from Claude, and now? Now he was not sure what he felt. Relief? Disappointment? Attraction? There was definitely attraction, but not on looks alone, for there were far prettier girls even around this table. Something about Amelia was drawing him in, and now that she had declared she had no interest in him, he could spend time with her without the worry of being trapped into marriage.

An image of standing at an altar with her flashed in his mind, but he took a large gulp of wine to rid himself of the thought. That was not what he wanted, he chanted to himself. He had been a smitten fool once; he was never going to allow himself to act that way again. No, he would enjoy Amelia's company, nothing more. But he couldn't deny that the thought of how her eyes sparkled when he made her smile had him looking forward to the coming days; the party had suddenly become far more appealing.

When the diners moved from the table, it was decided that the men would not retire to the billiard room for port and chat. Instead, Claude led Miss Simpson into the music room, clearly giving his mother a message that he would not willingly do as she asked. Richard offered his arm to Amelia, and she readily accepted it.

"Are you to be one of the young ladies to charm us with your musical talents tonight?" Richard asked, more than willing to continue his conversation with her. Amelia had entertained him throughout, and although she had flirted a little, she had laughed afterwards, taking away the cautiousness he would have normally felt when being teased. On more than one occasion, he had wondered why she was not married, for there seemed little wrong with her. A strange thought for one who was an expert at finding fault with every woman he met since Bea had hurt him.

"I suppose I must take a turn at some point, though I will hide at the back of the room with my friends in the hope that the younger ladies volunteer first."

"Is your musical ability so bad?" Richard was even more surprised that he wanted to tease her just as much as she seemed intent on quizzing him. He had not allowed himself to relax so much in anyone's company for a long time.

"The piano forte is not my friend, but I can play a tune or two on the harp."

"A good thing Aunt has a splendid harp just waiting to be used."

"It would be quite ungentlemanly to put me forward when it is clear I am happiest watching."

"Is it not all unmarried young ladies' desire to constantly show themselves off in a good light?"

"I hope not, for I am doomed to fail if that is the case!" Amelia said.

Richard laughed. "You tell many falsehoods, Miss Beckett."

"Oh," Amelia said as they entered the music room.

"Is there something amiss?" Richard asked, at first thinking she had taken umbrage at his words, but she was looking at the fireplace with a frown.

"No," she answered. "Just something has been moved, and it alters the symmetry of the ornaments, that is all. I love order in all things, and it grates when I see something odd, though I accept that makes me sound a very strange creature indeed."

"Not at all. I can see the comfort in order, and with your love of architecture, it makes even more sense."

Richard could not see anything missing, but in her distraction, he had led Amelia directly to the harp. "You brute," she whispered to him, but sat in the chair near the instrument; it would have been mulish to have openly objected.

Marie gave Richard a pointed look as he walked away from Amelia. He did not care. Whatever plans his aunt had, he was not going to be party to anything to do with getting Claude to agree to marry Amelia, especially since spending some time with her. He could not bear the thought of her nature being crushed by his cousin, for it was certain that would happen to her, for he was such a brute; those were his thoughts when trying to convince himself that it was natural he would feel protective of a visitor. There was no other motivation on his part, nor was his sickened feeling when thinking of them coupling anything other than natural concern, he insisted to himself.

Amelia played three songs, singing along, and received polite applause at the end of her recital. She smiled as she left the instrument, touching it with reverence as she walked by it to join the audience as the next young woman took her place.

"It is a beautiful instrument," Amelia said to Marie as she passed her, heading towards the back of the seating area.

"It is. I had hoped to have daughters to enjoy music with, but it was not to be," Marie said. "Feel free to come and play whenever you wish; the sound of music through the house is always pleasurable."

"Thank you."

"I believe you have younger sisters. Have they been presented yet?"

"No, they are a few years younger than I." Amelia was not sure that she covered her expression of surprise at such a change in subject.

"I always find it cruel that younger sisters are forced to wait until the elder ones are married," Marie said.

"I am sure that my parents will not hold them back for too long. There are some years between us, so they are not missing out too much."

"That is good to hear. Young girls should have every opportunity to shine, even better if they have a decent dowry to recommend them."

"I have no doubt they will be appreciated by those who meet them when it is their turn for a Season."

"It is useful when an older sibling makes a good match. Makes life easier for the whole family."

"There is no pressure from our parents on any of us to marry; they are content if we are happy."

"I always find life is happier when one has funds, for the opposite is nothing but a life of hardship and drudgery. Plus, if one can help other family members to prosper, all the better. Something an older sister should always remember."

"Perhaps. Please excuse me." Amelia moved away, not wishing the conversation to continue, and returned to her friends, bristling with indignation. "Of all the unsubtle hints I have ever received, that has to be the worst one."

"What did she say?" Patricia asked.

"Without actually saying the words, she suggested I needed to marry soon so that my sisters can have their come out, and I need to marry money so they can have reasonable dowries, and if I do not, I will remain poor and selfish."

"No!" Isabelle exclaimed.

"As if I would sacrifice myself to be married to her odious son, as much as I love my family," Amelia ground out. "Eldest daughters have enough to contend with; she did not need to remind me of the guilt I carry around."

"Your parents have never tried to force you to marry," Patricia said.

"No, but each time a new Season starts, Caroline and Lucy look at me in hope that this year will be the year I secure someone." Sometimes she wished her parents believed her reasoning that she could never face being married because of her scarring. She had tried to raise it on numerous occasions, but her words had been dismissed as her worrying too much.

"You missed your first three Seasons because of your injury," Isabelle said. "And then you could not dance when you did return. It is wonderful that you now can do everything you did before."

"Yes, learning to walk again took longer than I expected. At least now I give the appearance of not having this cursed injury." Amelia grimaced. "There was no one more frustrated than I that I did not recover quicker. Missing three full Seasons was not ideal, though it would not have affected anything in the end."

"People should not make assumptions when they do not know the facts," Patricia said.

"After Mrs. Greenwood's words, I suspect that I might be the one being considered by her as the sacrificial lamb," Amelia said.

"Then she does not know you!" Isabelle chuckled, making Amelia smile for the first time since her interaction with Marie.

"No. She certainly does not."

Chapter Four

An afternoon of games was arranged to take advantage of the fine weather they were enjoying. On the large lawn, a canopy was erected for anyone wishing to sit out of the sun, while other tables and chairs were scattered nearby.

A game of bowls was started with two teams led by Claude and Richard. It was clear that few guests wanted to join Claude, but unfortunately for the young ladies present, it was Marie who chose the teams. Patricia and Isabelle were placed on Richard's team, while Amelia was nominated for Claude's team, to neither's pleasure.

Marie's actions convinced Amelia even more that she was the one seen as persuadable into marrying Claude, but shrugged at her friends in acceptance of being on his team. Marriage was another thing entirely; she would never be so desperate, even without her scars.

Claude had scowled at his mother, but there were others on his team who he was clearly happy with. He spent the next ten minutes explaining the rules of the game with as much physical contact between whoever he was instructing and himself as he could get away with in front of the chaperones.

Turning to Amelia, he glowered at her. "I suppose you do not know how to play? If not, watch us and you can pick it up."

Amelia tried to stop the smile at Claude's words to her but could not. She saw a flicker of confusion at her reaction, but she said nothing, placing herself against a small wall at the edge of the lawned area. Too much standing would make her legs ache, and she had the impression that there would be a lot of hanging around while Claude tried to impress the younger members of the group.

It was not long before Richard came to stand nearby. "I hope you are ready to be defeated, Miss Beckett, for I take every competition I am involved with very seriously."

Amelia could not help laughing. "You say that with some arrogance, my lord, which is rather foolish when you have no idea of the abilities of the opponents you face."

"I have spent many afternoons on this very lawn playing bowls."

"I concur then that you might have the advantage on the lay of the land, but as for personal expertise, I should confess that bowls was one of the pastimes I could undertake whilst in my invalid chair."

Richard was taken aback that she had been so injured as to be unable to walk. When she had mentioned the injury from the horse, she had almost made light of it as if it was nothing much but had led her to a fear of horses; it seemed it had been a more severe incident. He admired the way she treated it with almost indifference, and he responded in kind. "Then it is to be a real game of challenge. I shall look forward to knocking any threat you try to create well and truly off the green."

"Confident words that you might live to regret, my lord."

Amelia watched as Richard walked away, taking control of his team and clearly giving them guidance in a pleasant but authoritative way. His manner was in marked contrast to Claude's, who was currently talking to just one of the team, and by the expression on Miss Wear's face, she was not enjoying the exchange. Amelia sighed when she glanced at the girl's parents, who seemed delighted that Claude was singling their daughter out. It was not how she thought parents should act when their daughter was clearly uncomfortable, but it was not her place to say or do anything. She pitied the girl.

When it was her turn to bowl, she was approached by Richard, who had clearly been speaking the truth when claiming to be very competitive; he stood close to anyone bowling, watching and commenting on their action. Smiling as she stood next to him, not intimidated in the slightest, she crouched, ready to take aim and bowl with precision. But she had reached lower than her legs were comfortable with, and as soon as she released the ball from her hand, she wobbled slightly as she tried to stand up.

Richard immediately reached out to steady her, and Amelia smiled at him with thanks. "I still forget that I do not have full use of my legs until I try to do something which stretches them too much. Thank you for the use of your arm. I appreciate it."

"Are you unwell? If you are in pain, I could help you to the house." Richard was immediately all concern for her.

"No, thank you. I assure you it is just that I forget my limitations sometimes; I have a little discomfort, but it is a mere trifle," Amelia said, warmed by his concern.

"When you first mentioned your injury when Miss Evans was being insensitive about your riding abilities, I had presumed you were no longer suffering." Richard stepped back so they did not get in the way of the next bowler but still allowed Amelia to hold on to his arm.

"Ah, yes. Everyone presumes it is due to a lack of money that I choose not to stable my own horse," Amelia said dryly, keeping away from the real question which had been intimated. "I suppose she was not to know, how did she put it, that I was maimed."

"It was a bad choice of words, and like myself, she made presumptions without knowing the facts, just as I have done with regard to your bowling ability. Now that I have had to suffer the embarrassment of watching you strike my ball off the lawn, I am happy to admit just how very foolish both myself and Miss Evans were. It did neither of us any benefit to show such a top lofty side to our personalities."

Smiling at his magnanimous attitude in defeat, she was pleased that her carefully aimed ball had knocked his clear away. She could not help raising her eyebrows, trying to move beyond speaking about her injury. "I can hardly believe the great Earl of Douglas is admitting he is as infallible as the rest of the little people."

Richard glared at her before answering. "Am I that much of a beast?"

"Only when you think yourself superior to a most excellent opponent," Amelia answered with a smile at the bark of laughter her words caused.

Enid sat next to her friend, looking over at Richard and Amelia, who were joining the others in the game once more. "You are playing a dangerous game with Amelia. Do not think I am not aware of what you are trying to do; you never were one for being subtle about what you wanted."

Marie narrowed her eyes. "I will be offering her the best chance she has at a good match. She will be well rewarded for taking on Claude."

"You underestimate the new generation, Marie. They want love, not money."

"Pah! You cannot live on love, but when you told me about her family situation, it fitted my scheme perfectly. She will be able to help her whole family and still have money to fritter away with what I will be offering her."

"When you asked me about her, I did not know what you were intent upon." Enid was angry with her friend for not being honest about their visit.

"Why do you think I invited the three of them?"

"I thought they might secure a husband. I did not understand that there would be so few gentlemen here, though Amelia and his lordship do seem to be getting on well."

"I wanted to see all Patricia's friends before I made my final decision. A pity two of them were unavailable, but from how you had spoken of her, and then almost from the moment I saw her, I knew

Amelia would be perfect for Claude," Marie said.

"They would not suit at all," Enid insisted.

"You think she would be more suited to Richard? I have seen that smile on your face as you've watched them, but you are wrong. He would never accept her. He might enjoy her company for a day or two, but he will not marry for anything but duty. He will certainly not be falling in love, if that is what she is hoping. He has been stung once before, and in that regard, his heart is as hard as his father's was."

Enid bristled on Amelia's behalf. "If he marries for status rather than a good match, a love match, then it is his loss. I am not presuming either of them for Amelia; I am saying you have chosen the wrong girl for your son. Look to one of the younger ones; it is clear Claude prefers them."

"Because he knows full well he will be able to bully them," Marie said.

"Then do not let him marry at all."

"He needs to be settled. The right woman will be the making of him. Why do Richard and you disbelieve what I say? I know my son, and I know what he needs."

"You might know Claude, though I still say your scheme is misguided, but you do not know Amelia."

"Are you going to tell her of my scheme?"

Enid sighed. She was torn, being of the mind that Claude was the type of man who should not marry anyone, but especially someone she was fond of. He had a cruel streak in him that she did not like. "I brought them here to enjoy two weeks with you, and yes, I thought one of them might attract one of many gentlemen I had presumed would be here, for they are all intelligent girls. I had no idea that you intended to have such an uneven number of guests. I will not admit that you are wishing for Amelia to make a match with Claude for the moment, but if you try anything untoward, I will be honest with her."

"I could be offended that you do not consider my son a worthy prize," Marie grumbled.

"Now you are doing it too brown!" Enid laughed. "You are prepared to bribe a young woman to get him a wife; that is how highly you think of him. Do not chide me for matching your low opinion."

Marie glowered. "If I did not love you so much, I would cast you off for being too honest."

"Someone has to try and keep you in line."

Whilst Enid was a grandmother, having married straight out of the schoolroom, Marie had married late, meaning there was little more than a few years between them. They had both lost their husbands around the same time, and a bond had quickly formed, which was deeper than other friendships of longer duration.

The pair continued to watch the bowling match with interest, noticing Claude reprimanding Amelia when she did not reach low enough over the ball to deliver it with the precision he wanted.

"What is he finding fault with now? It is supposed to be a chance for them to get to know each other," Marie grumbled.

"Perhaps he should take notice of what is being said around him," Enid replied. "She struggles with some movements because of an injury she has. It was clear she had issues when his lordship went to her aid. Claude should be aware that Amelia is not able to bend down fully with ease."

"Oh, blast the boy!" Marie cursed as Amelia swung around to face Claude, hands on hips. "What is going to happen now?"

Amelia had been cursed, shouted at, and ridiculed as the game had progressed; since first bending down, her legs had been throbbing in discomfort. She would have liked to have sat down, but had not wanted to spoil the game. Having borne Claude's comments, reprimands, and abuse with a semblance of grace until she tried to lower herself a little further to appease him, and she felt the discomfort of her scars being pulled in directions that hurt, she had had enough. "If you can do better, play the ball yourself," she snapped at Claude.

"All you need to do is bend lower!" Claude shouted in return. "Like this." Grabbing hold of Amelia's shoulders, he forced her downwards, not really caring that she would not be in the position for bowling; it was the action of a bully taking control.

Pain coursed through Amelia as she was pushed down at speed. She tried to grab onto Claude to prevent her downward movement, but he was too strong and had the advantage of surprise. She cried out in pain, collapsing on the ground and writhing in agony.

"Oh, get up!" Claude snapped. "Enough of the dramatics!"

Claude was bodily pushed out of the way, losing his balance and falling heavily on his rear, letting out a roar of protest. His two friends ran to his aid, but Richard ignored the impact his actions had caused his cousin as he crouched by Amelia's side.

"Miss Beckett, what is wrong? Is it your legs?"

Amelia was white and swallowing convulsively. "Yes," she managed to whisper.

Patricia and Isabelle were only steps behind Richard. "She has scarring and struggles to bend the leg without pain," Patricia said quietly. "Being forced as she was could have done some damage to them."

"No, I will be well," Amelia said, but she was turning green. "Oh dear." Turning to the side, she cast up her accounts, making everyone else who had crowded around jump back in disgust except Richard, Patricia, and Isabelle.

Enid joined the group. "Does she need a doctor?"

"Yes," Richard said, not looking up, but stroking Amelia's back as she retched.

Amelia had tried to shake her head at Enid's words, but Isabelle placed a hand on her shoulder. "You need to be checked by someone. We have not seen you in so much pain in a long time."

"Sudden," Amelia choked out.

"I did not know she was deformed!" Claude whined behind the

group. "How was I to know?"

"Claude, come out of the way and stop making things worse!" Marie snapped at her son. "I have sent a servant for the doctor. She needs to be carried to her chamber to make her more comfortable."

Two footmen lifted Amelia from the ground, the movement causing her to moan before falling into a dead faint. Richard swung around, furious that he had been forced to stand by because of etiquette and allow the footmen to carry Amelia into the house when the urge to be the one caring for her almost took his breath away. At Claude's words, Richard redirected his frustration and anger at the person who had caused Amelia so much pain. Storming over to his cousin, who for once had done as his mother said by moving away, Richard planted a facer on him before Claude had any time to react.

"You absolute idiot! You were there when she said she had injuries. It is about time you took notice of something other than your own selfish needs. You disgust me," Richard snarled at him. Not waiting for a reply from Claude, who had yelped and was now holding a handkerchief to his bloody nose, Richard marched across the lawn to catch up with the party surrounding Amelia.

"He will pay for that!" Claude hissed, though his voice was nasal because of the injury.

"A shocking display in all regards," Mrs. Evans said, crossing the lawn to be closer to Claude, her daughters flanking her on either side. "You as the gentleman of the house, too. It shows a distinct lack of respect on the earl's part, I am very disappointed in his actions. As you said, how were you to know? Miss Beckett had mentioned some sort of injury, but who listens to such crude topics when discussed at the breakfast table?"

"Precisely," Claude said mulishly. "Richard has always been the same, thinking he has more authority than me because of his title, but his father cast him off, and if it was not for us, then he would have been homeless. It is a pity he chooses to forget that and shows no respect for what I have done for him."

"You have clearly been nothing but kind towards him, and this is how he repays you. It is utterly disgraceful that he should act in such a brutish way," Mrs. Evans continued. "Would you like us to accompany you to the house, and we can arrange some ice and perhaps a little brandy to help with the pain? I really would not like to leave you alone, for though you are a fine, strong young man, that was a brutal attack."

As Marie had deserted her son along with the others, Claude inclined his head as if he was bestowing a great privilege on the Evans women. "That would be very kind of you. I would have drawn his cork if he had not moved away so quickly; his actions were not that of a gentleman."

"Precisely. I must say, I am shocked that the earl is allowed to get away with such a high-handed attitude, yet your mother seemed not to care. Come with us; we will look after you as you should be. Laura, Sarah, take Mr. Greenwood's arms. I know he is a very capable young man, but being prone to worry about those I care about, I would be happier if you were on either side of him to make sure he can lean on you if needed," Mrs. Evans instructed, and leading the way to the house, she looked positively joyful at the way the situation had played out.

The other families, who had witnessed everything but had not gone ahead with the party surrounding Amelia or followed Claude, began to disperse, making their way slowly back to the house. A few looked out of sorts, and there were some urgent mutterings between mothers and daughters as they walked.

∞

AMELIA AWOKE TO a cool cloth on her forehead and the worst headache she had experienced in a long time. The throb in her leg made her feel queasy again, but there was nothing left in her stomach, so she swallowed the feelings of nausea and kept her eyes closed.

"The doctor should be here soon," Patricia whispered, stroking Amelia's hand.

Amelia nodded slightly, but squeezed her eyes shut when the movement caused her head to swim.

"Stay still. You know you will not get any relief until the doctor gives you laudanum and your legs are rested," Isabelle said, replacing the cool cloth with another.

A knock on the door indicated the arrival of the doctor, and after Patricia had given him some background information, he examined Amelia. She had winced, but had not opened her eyes, nor said a word while the doctor was checking her legs over. Eventually, he placed the sheets gently over her once more.

"From what you say has happened previously, the pain should ease quite quickly, but I will give you some laudanum for the next few days. You probably know better than I how to treat a setback like this and what rest is needed. From the look of things, you have not caused any long-lasting damage."

"That is good to know," Patricia said with a sigh of relief. "If she had to go through the pain of those first couple of years..."

"I can only imagine the recovery needed from the injuries. I am presuming that you were lucky to survive such an attack," the doctor said to Amelia.

Amelia nodded her head slightly.

"Give her this draught immediately and then another when she wakes up. Before giving her the third dose, let her come round a little and see if the pain has eased enough to be bearable. If it is still too painful, give her the final draught and call me back." Once his instructions were given and he had seen Amelia take the first cup of liquid, he said his goodbyes before leaving the room.

"Poor Amelia," Patricia said as Amelia drifted asleep. "She did not deserve such rough treatment."

"He is an absolute cad for doing what he did," Isabelle said.

"I am no longer wary about that ogre of a man. If I see him, he will get a piece of my mind. I cannot explain how angry I am that she has to suffer. Why the devil didn't Mrs. Greenwood put us on her son's team?"

"Because she wants Amelia to be his wife."

"There was never going to be any chance of that; she should have perceived that when talking to Amelia. I hope she accepts it now," Patricia said. "Or it will not be just the son I curse to the devil."

"You sound like Amelia." Isabelle smiled.

"One of us has to pick up the mantle whilst she is indisposed."

"Oh lord!" Isabelle groaned.

Chapter Five

RICHARD PACED THE library. He had never felt anger like it when Claude had grabbed Amelia and forced her to the ground. Not grasping that Claude would hurt her old injury, Richard had already started to move to stop Claude from being so brutish. When Amelia had let out the cry of pain, he had never felt a sound cut through him as that had. It would be absurd to say that he felt her pain, but he certainly understood that Claude had hurt her severely, and that increased his rage.

Knocking his cousin away from her would have caused him some satisfaction if he had thought to look behind him to see Claude floundering like some upside-down crab until he was hauled to his feet by his friends. Richard's complete focus had been on reaching Amelia and trying in some feeble way to help her.

Now he was alone while everyone else seemed to be attending to her, and though he knew he had no right to feel the way he did, he wanted to be by her side.

Cursing himself, he turned once more and strode to the other side of the fireplace. She was annoying, opinionated, and clearly brought up in the same way as her wild brother, but there was something about her that he could not ignore. Why did he want to be by her side, demanding that the doctor take the pain away? He had never worried about someone as he was doing now, and he barely knew her!

Pausing, he was struck by a thought. Had he worried over Bea? He had wanted her to be comfortable in all situations, but had he ached to be beside her? Shaking his head in disgust at himself, he continued his pacing. Bea had never been ill, but if she had been, of course he would have been even more anxious about her. Amelia was a virtual stranger, and it was just a natural concern for her welfare, that was all. Closing his eyes for a moment, he silently chanted that she was a guest of his aunt and meant nothing to him.

Enid interrupted his pacing by entering the library. "I am looking for Marie," she said, her tone serious.

"I thought she would be with Miss Beckett."

"No."

"In that case, I hope she is tearing a strip off my cousin."

"She will not be the only one in that regard. If you see her, please inform her that three of the families are leaving as soon as they are packed."

"How is Miss Beckett? She is all that I am concerned about. I do not give a damn about who goes and who stays. In fact, if everyone left, it would bring this farce to an end."

"She is sleeping now. The doctor thinks that a few days of complete rest will allow the pain from her scars to ease. We will know if there has been any permanent damage after these next days have passed, though the doctor is hopeful that there isn't."

Richard winced at Enid's explanation. "I could kill him."

"You and me both," Enid agreed. "She has been through so much and fought so hard to walk again, and I only know with Patricia telling me about Amelia's struggles; Amelia rarely mentions anything herself, but that girl has suffered greatly. If this has caused irreparable damage…well, let us just wait and see, but there will be consequences for Claude if this has."

"Whatever she needs will be provided," Richard said. He was panicked at the thought that Amelia might be permanently hurt. Not in the way Claude would recoil from someone he did not consider as perfect a specimen as himself, but that a woman so full of life might be confined in what she could do. The regret that he would never have the opportunity of dancing with her flitted through his mind, and he gritted his teeth at his own selfish and unexpected thought. "She mentioned that she was restricted to an invalid chair for some time. Do you think she will need one?"

"I have no idea until she has had time to rest. She was in one for two years and then could only walk with support for another year. I would hate to see her return to that state. They told her she would never walk again, but she was determined to prove the doctors wrong," Enid said.

Richard's lips twitched. "You do not surprise me."

"No, nor anyone who truly knows her, but I am sure she had her moments of doubt, whereas your cousin, when I find him, will be under no doubt about what I think of him."

"I almost pity him, but not quite. If you need my assistance, just say the word, and I will make him truly sorry for what he has caused."

"Do not worry. He will think the cursing from his mother was a gentle telling off when I have finished with him."

Enid left the room, and Richard resumed his pacing. Amelia had suffered so much, which made what had happened even more appalling. He paused once more in thought. When he was young, he had been helpless to change anything about his situation. It had taken his aunt to come and sort out his unhappy home life. Then, after everything that happened with Bea, it had reinforced the sense of loneliness he carried within him. Once more, he was helpless and at a loss for what to do for the best. He was as ineffective as the neglected little boy and the love-struck young man had been.

Placing his hands on the mantelpiece and hanging his head, he growled in frustration. She had to be well. She just had to.

ON THE THIRD day, Amelia was feeling well enough to receive visitors, or so she thought. After a visit from Miss Wear and her parents, who wanted to go over the shocking event in great detail, and then another from Miss King and her parents, who wished to do exactly the same, she groaned when told that Claude's two friends, Albert and Freddie, were outside the door.

"Do I have to see them? I barely know them, and I am in my bed," Amelia whispered to her friends.

"I will dissuade them from a visit," Patricia said, immediately going to the door of their shared chamber.

When Patricia spoke to Albert and Freddie, Amelia was relieved to hear their protestations.

"Oh no, we don't want to come in!" Freddie exclaimed quickly after Patricia had explained that Amelia was feeling tired. "I get a funny feeling in my insides if I have to visit a sick room. Makes me go all queer, it does. We have been to the village and bought Miss Beckett some cakes and some fruit jellies. Thought it would be just the thing to help forget all that happened."

"A rough day, but best forget about it, eh?" Albert said quickly. "Claude was a little overexcited. No harm done, eh?"

Amelia watched as Patricia's posture stiffened, and she spoke quickly before her friend could respond. "Please thank the gentlemen; the treats are much appreciated."

Patricia swung around to glare at Amelia, but she accepted the two large boxes, and thanking them through gritted teeth, she closed the door. "I should have said..."

Amelia smiled. "It is not their fault, and they were clearly very uncomfortable."

"And so they should be, having chosen the worst kind of friend."

"At least we have treats," Amelia said before groaning at yet another knock at the door.

This time, Mrs. Evans was seeking entry with her daughters. They had been out in the meadow and collected some flowers. "I always think wildflowers are so much prettier than those grown in the hothouse," Mrs. Evans said. "Shall I put them here for you?" They were already in a vase, and she walked over to the dressing table near Isabelle's bed where Amelia could see them clearly.

"Thank you, it is very kind of you," Amelia said. "Everyone is being very thoughtful."

"Did I not tell you girls that Miss Beckett would be magnanimous and not join with Mrs. Greenwood in constantly scolding Mr. Greenwood," Mrs. Evans said to her daughters.

"Mr. Greenwood has been very upset, for his mother says wicked things to him no matter who is in his company. He is saying he will return to London if she does not stop."

"I can understand Mrs. Greenwood's actions, for he did behave badly," Isabelle said, surprising her two friends that she had spoken, for she was the one who always tried to avoid conflict.

"The problem was that Miss Beckett did not make it clear that she was not normal. Any one of us could have hurt her because of her silence on the matter," Mrs. Evans said.

"Not normal?" Amelia choked out.

"Would you have liked to see one of your daughters treated so roughly by Mr. Greenwood?" Patricia demanded.

"Neither of my girls would have played the game so poorly," Mrs. Evans answered.

"I suddenly feel very tired," Amelia said.

"Just one more visit," Marie said, entering the room with a very sullen Claude at her heels. The Evans family stepped away from the bed, but even though Marie shot them a look, they did not leave the room.

"It feels a little crowded in here," Amelia said dryly.

"This will not take long," Marie said. "Claude!"

"I am sorry for what I did, and I hope you will allow me to make it up to you when you are well enough to get up and about." If he had been reading the words from a piece of paper, they would have sounded less stilted, and the three friends tried to hide their amusement despite what he had caused.

Amelia looked at Marie. "What did you threaten him with for him to agree to ask for my forgiveness?"

Marie narrowed her eyes at Amelia. "I knew you were perfect."

Both Claude and Amelia exclaimed at her words, but Claude was the loudest. "I am not marrying her! I want to make my own choices in life!" As he stormed out of the room, Mrs. Evans and her daughters followed him, mumbling their excuses.

Amelia looked at Marie. "I will not be marrying your son."

"I will make you an offer that you will not be able to refuse," Marie said belligerently. "You need funds, and I can give you more than you will ever need."

"As tempting as that might be," Amelia said sarcastically, "I am not prepared to sell myself to get married to a man who clearly cannot abide me."

"He would grow to like you."

Amelia laughed. "The same cannot be said for me with regards to him. I will never marry a man who I cannot stand to be in the company of, no matter what the incentives are. I am sorry if my words offend you. I will, of course, leave as soon as I am able to."

"There is no need," Marie said. "You must only go when you are fit to travel, even if it takes longer than the two weeks you were due to stay. At least we can do one thing right, which is send you back when you have fully recovered."

"Thank you, but I will not change my mind if that is what you are hoping for."

"Even if I offer everything you could ever want?"

"You do not know what I want," Amelia said. She could curse herself for thinking of Richard at that moment, for he had not been near her since the accident. He was probably of the same mind as Claude, disgusted with someone who was not perfect. The thought depressed her.

"Usually, we want our families to be happy," Marie said.

"Not at the cost of my own happiness," Amelia pointed out. "My parents would never agree to my marrying on such terms as you offer."

"Then you are going to remain a spinster."

"Probably, but I had already accepted that a long time ago. It is a thought that does not worry me as much as it seems to worry others."

"Remember those words when you are twenty years older and your family dreads your visits. It is one thing to be principled when you are young and have a home, but when your parents are gone, your life will not be so secure," Marie said before sighing at the looks of astonishment she received from the three women. "I had to try. I will mention the subject no more, but I meant what I said when I promised that you are welcome here for as long as you need."

"Thank you," Amelia said. Marie nodded and left the room, leaving the three friends alone. "Oh my word! What an afternoon! I am drained!"

"As much as I would like to talk over the outrageousness of each of the visits, I think you should close your eyes and try and get some sleep," Patricia said.

"There will be no need to try. I just hope I do not have nightmares about being married to Claude."

"We will stay to wake you if needed," Isabelle said, sitting next to the bed.

"Thank you," Amelia said, her eyes already closing.

Chapter Six

It had been four days, but he was finally going to see her. Having stopped the butler carrying two walking sticks to Amelia's room, he had an excuse to knock on the door. Sending flowers had not eased the need to spend time with her; he wanted confirmation from her to ensure she was recovering and that she lacked nothing.

Knocking on the door, he was invited in by Patricia. "Ahh, here are your walking aids, Amelia," Patricia said over her shoulder. "I can take them, my lord."

"There is no need. I will accompany Miss Beckett downstairs if she feels well enough to join everyone for luncheon," Richard said. Now that he had entered the room, he could breathe a little easier; Amelia looked bright and alert. Yes, she was pale, but her eyes were shining, though they looked at him with a strange expression that he could not fathom. Not dwelling on anything other than she looked far better than when she was brought in, he felt an easing of the tightness in his chest, which had started the moment she had been attacked by Claude. He had not been aware of, until seeing her, just how tensely he had been holding himself.

"I would like to leave my chamber, though I have had the best companions." Amelia smiled at her friends. "I have to warn you, my lord, it will be a slow process."

"I am at your disposal. You can set the pace, and I will not berate you, even once."

Amelia smiled. "In that case, if you could call back in fifteen minutes, I should be ready to go."

Richard bowed and left the room. Instead of retreating downstairs, he waited at the top of the stairs until Patricia opened the door, and although she looked a little surprised that he had loitered, she indicated that he should join them once more.

"Are you ready, Miss Beckett?"

"Yes. I never thought a journey to the dining room would feel like such an adventure. I have been stationary too long."

"I think you had a valid reason," Isabelle said.

"It does not alter the fact that it feels as if I am wasting my days." Amelia stood up with Richard's help, smiling gratefully at him as he took her weight as she readied herself with the walking sticks. "Ready whenever you are, my lord."

The pair walked slowly out of the room, Richard constantly checking that Amelia was feeling as comfortable as she could be. After the sixth time of asking over a space of about ten steps, Amelia stopped.

"I have been through this before," she said, amused but grateful for his concern.

"Not at the hands of my buffoon of a cousin," Richard growled out.

"True, but at least this time the recovery should be faster."

"Was it a long period before you healed when it first happened?"

Amelia sighed. "I was due to have my first Season, and I thought I was invincible when I approached a horse my father had just purchased. It was well known for being a bad-tempered brute, but I was too arrogant to listen. By the end of the day, I regretted my overconfidence."

"We are all guilty of thinking we know best, especially when first out of the schoolroom."

"That sounds like a confession to me." Amelia smiled, but she continued before he could respond. "In that instance, I certainly didn't.

They said I was lucky to survive the attack. I have very little memory of it, but I was told he just kept biting again and again. It was only when two stable hands attacked him with pitchforks that he stopped, and they were able to drag me away."

"It sounds horrific."

"Yes, I am glad I cannot remember most of it." They were at the top of the stairs, and Amelia paused. "I can use the banister and one of my sticks to get myself down if you would be good enough to carry the other?"

"I would prefer to hold both sticks, and you can use my arm and the banister to lean on," Richard said. "I know I am but a weak and feeble dandy, but I think even I can bear your weight."

"As if I would dare to call you a dandy! You must be a Corinthian at least!" Amelia laughed, but handed both walking sticks over.

"I don't like to boast," Richard said as they started a slow descent. "How long did it take to recover?"

"I suppose I have not really fully recovered; you saw how I wobbled the other day." Amelia grimaced. "But it was two years before I could walk, then a year relearning how to do everything, and then I could start learning to dance, though I am not able to take part in every dance, especially not the more energetic ones. It is a good thing I spend my time on the wallflower benches."

"Your come out was delayed by four years?"

"More or less. I was actually out after the third year but could only attend certain events. I still suffered from tiredness, even though I could not take part fully."

"It must have frustrated you to be on the sideline of everything."

"I missed the dancing. I loved to dance, but what was the use of repining over something I could not change? I had to be realistic; by the time I was able to take part more fully in society, my time for securing a match had passed. Even the most optimistic of us know that three or four Seasons worth of debutantes will tip the odds against an heiress, let alone a woman with only a small dowry and who struggles to move sometimes."

Richard admired how matter-of-fact she was. He wasn't sure he could sound completely at ease with the way she had been cheated out of the best years of her life and the potential to gain a husband. It probably explained why he had never crossed paths with her; even the debutantes with the smallest dowries tried to be introduced to the aristocracy. He was quiet as he mused what she must have endured, admiring the fact that she was still so spirited. All thoughts of ill-feeling because of her comments about his quizzing glass were well and truly forgotten.

"Ah, it is always a relief to reach the bottom of the stairs," Amelia said. "Stretching the legs is still quite painful."

"Do you need to rest for a little while?" Patricia asked. Both she and Isabelle had been following the descent.

"I think it would be a good idea," Amelia said, grateful that Richard immediately ordered a footman to bring a chair. Sitting down, she sighed in relief. "I am a poor specimen."

"You are one of the strongest people I know," Richard said. His hand was on the back of the chair in a protective gesture.

"Thank you. I doubt I will feel strong when I hobble into the dining room while everyone is already seated." They could hear voices from behind the closed door.

"The group is smaller than usual, as Claude has taken the men out for a day's sport," Richard said.

"Oh, has he? There is some comfort that I will not see him, but should you not be with them? Am I delaying you?"

"Not at all. I am not my cousin's best-loved person at the moment; something about how I might have ruined his good looks forever. I did ask him whether he had ever peered into a looking glass before I drew his cork and pointed out that my actions could only have improved matters. He should be thanking me. I am quite surprised at the cursing caused by my observations. I have never noticed how florid my cousin becomes when he is angry; it is a most unflattering look."

Amelia laughed. "I expect you gave the set-down whilst glaring through your quizzing glass?"

"Of course," Richard said. "One has to try to keep Claude under control."

"Good luck with that," Amelia muttered as she rose from the seat, Richard immediately by her side.

Richard helped Amelia to her seat in the dining room, which was to the right of his aunt at Marie's insistence. He did not want to leave Amelia's side but was fully aware that everyone would be watching him closely. Gentlemanlike attention was acceptable, but any sign of partiality was certainly to be avoided. Worrying about her was one thing, raising speculation was another thing entirely. No matter that they'd already had a conversation about marriage; others did not know that.

Mrs. Evans sat next to Richard and was very cool towards him, which suited them both. Richard mulled over what Amelia had revealed. He admired her more than he would normally allow himself to do, and that was before hearing of the reality of her struggles. Now, he wanted even more to be the one to protect her, look after her, and keep her shielded from the world's troubles. This was a dangerous position to be in, and he was torn and confused by such inappropriate emotions. He tried to convince himself that it was nothing more than he pitied the woman. He had been brought up to be a gentleman, and it was purely feelings of decency that were confusing him.

Half of him wished to be by her side, the other half wanted to run in the opposite direction and never see Amelia again. He knew he had a real problem, and he did not know which was the more frightening: being attracted to someone after so endlessly longing for Bea, or the risk of being rejected again.

As they ate, he watched her chatting happily to his aunt. She really could fit in wherever she was, something he had always struggled with, titled gentleman or not. Pausing his fork halfway to his mouth, he knew the moment something was wrong. Her bearing changed, her posture stiffening and her face becoming rigid. Resisting the urge to rush to her side, Richard watched with increasing concern, not helped by the glare shot in his direction from Amelia, who, this morning at least, had been all smiles towards him. He had no idea what his aunt was saying, but he knew without doubt that he was not going to like it.

∽

AMELIA HAD ENJOYED the first part of the meal. Patricia and Isabelle had been wonderful nurses over the last few days, but she was not one who liked being restricted, so it was with pleasure that she sat next to Marie, expecting to be entertained by the forthright, acerbic woman.

Marie had been apologetic initially about what had happened, but it was not long before she was her usual self and had started to tease Amelia. "I wanted to invite all of your friends to this gathering, but Enid said two of you were unavailable."

"That would have been a lot of single women," Amelia said.

"Yes. I told Richard when he complained of being surrounded by wallflowers that he need not worry about my having any plans in pairing him up with any of you. It seemed to make him accept remaining here when I explained that I was hoping to choose one of you for my son, but I needed Claude to feel like he had a choice of a bride. I promised Richard that there would be enough younger women for him to choose from. You do not mind my being so open with you? Now that you have been clear in your refusal, I think there is no need to pretend that I had not gathered everyone here for a purpose."

"I appreciate your being candid," Amelia said stiffly. "It helps me to see how things really are." She was stinging from the fact that Richard had been derogatory towards her friends and herself before he had even met them. It was so typical a reaction of the man she had thought he was, not the man she now thought so highly of and was constantly in her mind.

"That is what I thought," Marie said. "I will still welcome you into the family if you should change your mind, but that is the last I will say on the matter. I had hoped to marry both Claude and Richard off during this party, but neither is being cooperative."

"I suppose they have their own ideas of what they would wish for in a wife and want to feel they had chosen themselves. I doubt my brother would welcome any interference from my parents. I know I would not."

"Richard tried telling me that from the start, but I promised I would not meddle too much where he was concerned. He is more likely to make a good choice once he can put his past to rest."

"Oh?"

"It is as Enid said, young ones today want to fall in love before they marry. Pfft, he fell in love, and she was a great disappointment. I do not understand the need for a love match; my own marriage was one of convenience initially, but I could not have cared more for my husband if I had chosen him myself."

"You were very fortunate in that regard."

"Love was an addition I would not have missed if it had not been there," Marie continued conversationally while watching what was going on across the table.

"Again, I would say that you were lucky not to feel the need for love." Amelia was stiff with annoyance, wanting to remove herself from the room, the house, but unable to do so. She hated being so helpless, for she could not leave the table without help, and the man who would be first to her aid was the one person she wanted to get away from.

"I am surprised to find you are a romantic."

"You seem to have formed very firm opinions of me without any foundation or real knowledge of my personality or wishes."

"True, and perhaps I should not have done so, but you cannot fault me in coming to the conclusion that you are probably the only one in the room who would be the perfect match for Claude."

Amelia tried to stifle the grimace, but was not convinced she had succeeded, so looked across the table as Marie was doing. She had already sent a glare towards Richard when his aunt had confessed he had ridiculed her and her friends, but she sent him another dark look for good measure.

Marie noticed the direction of Amelia's gaze. "My nephew looks at Miss Evans a lot."

"Does he? You might be wishing him happy yet," Amelia said, taking a gulp of wine to try to remove the bitter taste in her mouth.

"Oh, I do not think he would align himself with her. I only invited those three to spread the ages of the girls I had invited. It was Miss Jones or Miss Simpson I was hoping he would marry. I am fully aware that he needs a compliant, meek wife, someone he would trust never to let him down as Bea did. Either one of those two would have been perfect. I could have cursed Claude to the devil for spending as much time with the girls as he could, and now they have left without Richard hardly speaking to them. It has been such a wasted opportunity."

"I am sure he could follow them to London or wherever they have gone," Amelia said. "Mrs. Greenwood, would you excuse me? I feel a little tired; if you do not mind, I would like to return to my chamber."

"Of course, you do whatever you need to do." Marie indicated to a footman to help Amelia, but Richard immediately left his seat and approached his aunt and Amelia.

"Miss Beckett, please allow me to escort you," he said, offering his arm.

"No, thank you, I am perfectly fine," Amelia snapped.

A little taken aback at the tone of her rebuttal, Richard followed her out of the dining room. Only when the door had closed did he speak as Amelia used the arm of the footman for support.

"Have I upset you, Miss Beckett? I would be sorry to hear that I have erred in your opinion."

"No, not at all. It is I who has been wrong," Amelia said, tone icy. "Please excuse me, my lord. I think it is best that you return to your aunt's guests. She told me how much you like to be in the company of someone who is meek and compliant. I am now surprised that we were able to have one civil conversation, let alone several of them, especially given how much you repined the fact that there were wallflowers invited to your party."

Richard stood still, rubbing his hand over his face in frustration. "My blasted aunt," he muttered.

"Do not chastise her for what she said. As she pointed out, it is best to be open and honest." Starting up the stairs, she did not look back at Richard, just concentrated on taking a step at a time, wishing that she had remained in her chamber. She was oblivious to Richard's turmoil as he watched her lean on a stranger as she struggled up the stairs.

She had been a fool of the highest order, and she cursed the way she had ignored what she had been told about him, instead, believing that he was someone who was better than he was, and what hurt the most, someone she was drawn to as she had not been drawn before.

It would be a long time before she trusted her instincts again, and it would be even longer before she would be able to look at him with equanimity.

Chapter Seven

THE LUNCH HAD tired Amelia emotionally and physically, so she was not lying when she begged to be excused from joining everyone during the evening. Insisting that Isabelle and Patricia left her to sleep, she watched as they readied themselves for supper.

"I think Grandmamma is regretting bringing us," Patricia said, pulling on her gloves when the maid had left them alone. "She was cursing Mrs. Greenwood to the devil this afternoon when I told her what she had revealed to you."

"I still think it was her way of warning you off her nephew," Isabelle said, rummaging on the dressing table. "The way he looks at you makes it clear that he finds you irresistible."

"Pfft! He is probably feeling sorry for his cousin in case I was persuaded to marry him," Amelia responded. "Then he would be permanently related to a woman who had been a wallflower! Oh, the shame of it!" She was teasing, but there was bitterness in her tone which she could not hide; it was because of her own foolishness she could not confess to her friends.

"I would not condemn him without speaking to him first," Isabelle cautioned.

"Too late." Amelia smiled. "Isabelle, what are you doing?"

Isabelle paused in her rummaging. "I cannot find my bracelet. You know, the blue one? I seem to have misplaced it, and I have no idea where it could be. I could have sworn I left it here when I took it off the night before the bowling match."

"Perhaps Mary put it in one of the drawers," Patricia suggested, moving over to help in the search.

"No, I have asked her about it and she said she had not seen it. Never mind, I am sure it will turn up. I probably should not wear it anyway. I fiddle with it when I am nervous."

"There is no need for you to be anxious." Amelia smiled at her friend.

"I am just concerned that Mrs. Greenwood will turn her attention to one of us now that you have refused to bow to her wishes. Not that I wished you to be forced into marriage, of course." Isabelle grinned, picking up her fan.

"Glad to hear it," Amelia said. "I think you are safe. Mrs. Greenwood wants a loud-mouthed fishwife by the sounds of it. You do not fit her requirements, whereas I am perfect."

"In that case, if you need anything, just shout." Patricia grinned. "We will hear you all the way in the dining room."

"Be gone!" Amelia laughed, falling back on her pillows with a sigh when she was left alone. He had insulted her, been typical of his class, and yet she could not stop thinking about him. Blast him to the devil!

RICHARD WAS IN a foul mood. The moment Patricia and Isabelle walked into the drawing room without Amelia, he had known he could not fix whatever his aunt had said to upset her.

Crossing to Patricia and Isabelle, he bowed. "Is Miss Beckett unwell?"

"She is tired from the exertions at luncheon," Patricia said coolly. "She needs to rest."

"Ah, I see. Does she require anything?"

"No."

"If she does, please let me know immediately." It was clear that they had been told of the conversation between Amelia and his aunt; both women had been civil to him thus far, but they were distinctly aloof now.

"I am sure there will be no need," Patricia said.

"She likes to read," Isabelle blurted out, turning pink at the way she had spoken. Gaining more control of herself, she continued. "And we have not had the chance to choose anything from the library. If you could send her something suitable to read…"

"Consider it done." Richard bowed and moved away.

"What did you say that for?" Patricia hissed as they joined the Misses Evans.

"Notice how he has not gone to a footman and given him instructions to take books to her?" Isabelle pointed out. "He is smitten, and I think Amelia is too. She would not have been so upset at careless words said before we had even met him if she did not wish him to think well of her."

"He was rude."

"Yes, but so were we. Remember we were laughing at him and his quizzing glass; that was rude too."

"You are far too sensible."

"That is not a recommendation I welcome; it would suggest boring," Isabelle groaned.

"Not at all. You have seen what I have not. I will be observing more now, that is for sure. Miss Evans, how are you?" Patricia said, sitting on the sofa.

Richard had returned to the decanter after speaking to Amelia's friends. Cursing the fact that he would have to sit through a long and tedious meal before he could escape to the library to choose some books for her, he poured a large amount of brandy.

Disturbed from his thoughts by Claude's friends, he did not hide his usual disdainful glower when Freddie spoke.

Seeming to be oblivious to Richard's unwelcoming manner, Freddie filled his own glass. "Claude has found out that there is to be a mill in the next village tonight. We need to be released from our duties here early."

"And why would I be interested in that?" Richard drawled.

"Claude said that his mother would accept whatever you said to excuse us. Of course, that means you are invited too," Freddie said hurriedly.

"I am glad to see though I am in his bad books, he can still find a use for me," Richard said, sipping his brandy.

"You will do it?" Albert asked eagerly. "I could do with an evening away from this tense atmosphere. It is all too strained, but Claude won't let us return to London."

Richard was not surprised that Claude controlled his friends. He needed to be top dog in everything he did, though his mother often thwarted him. Bullying people was easier than trying to be the son Marie wanted. "I will explain to Aunt that the gentlemen need an evening of sport, but that we will dance with the ladies tomorrow night."

"Oh." Albert was deflated.

"Take it or leave it, gentlemen. We cannot abandon the ladies without making amends for it another time. This is supposed to be a house party, after all."

"Half the people have gone," Freddie pointed out.

"Which is why you need to be particularly charming to the ones left behind." Richard was glad he did not practice what he preached, for he had been withdrawn since Amelia's accident. "Dancing tomorrow, or I do not make your excuses."

"Fine," Albert conceded.

"Does this mean you are joining us?" Freddie glanced at Claude as he uttered the words.

Richard almost suppressed the smile. "I have half a mind to join you just to annoy my cousin, but I have pressing matters of my own to attend to."

"Oh. Right. Good."

The men bowed and walked away, and Richard watched them speaking to Claude, telling him the good news. He wondered if his cousin would acknowledge the good deed he was doing for him, but was amused when Claude shrugged his shoulders and purposely did not look in Richard's direction.

It was amusing rather than an insult for Richard, and draining his glass, he walked to his aunt. She would not be pleased, but hopefully, the promise of a night of dancing would pacify her.

At the knock on her door, Amelia shouted to enter, but pulled her blanket higher when it was Richard who opened the door.

"My lord, I was not expecting you," she said coolly, cheeks flushing at the thought of him seeing her in her nightgown, hair around her shoulders.

Richard faltered a little. Why he had not considered her state of dress, he had no idea, but her face framed by a fall of auburn curls, contrasting against the white frill of her nightgown, made him think he had never seen anything so beautiful in his life. He had thought her handsome, but now, now she was stunning in his eyes.

Swallowing against the dryness of his throat, he bowed his head in greeting. "I beg pardon for disturbing you, but I have brought a selection of books I thought you might like."

"Oh. Thank you, that is very kind." Amelia was thrown at the gesture and the hesitancy he was suffering from.

"You were missed this evening."

"Was I?"

"Yes."

The silence stretched between them. For the first time, Amelia noticed that his eyes were not their usual ice blue, but warmer as he looked at her. That it was clearly a result of her being in bed made her skin prickle.

Eventually, she could stand the silence no longer. "If you could leave the books on the chest of drawers, please."

"What? Oh, yes, of course. There is to be dancing tomorrow evening."

"I doubt I will be doing any dancing." Amelia's tone returned to its coolness. "I suppose I am required to provide the music?"

"No, er, I suppose so," Richard faltered. "I thought it would be nice for you to watch."

Amelia let out a sharp laugh. "I do that regularly enough on the *wallflower* benches, my lord. I think I would prefer to remain here and read."

"Have I upset you, Miss Beckett?" Richard had finally come to his senses enough to know that whatever he had expected at his entrance to her chamber, this was not it. Not that he had thought there would be anything but a civil acknowledgment of his gesture, but she was being chilly at best.

"Have you, my lord? I am surprised you are even bothered enough to ask."

"I do not understand your meaning."

"No, you probably do not. 'Complaining of being surrounded by wallflowers, happy to know they were invited not for him but for his cousin' I think were more or less the words that your aunt used when describing your reaction to her visitors." Did she feel satisfaction or disappointment when he closed his eyes in an admission that he had indeed said something along the lines his aunt had said? Amelia wasn't quite sure, only that the lead in her chest increased when he did not deny the comment, proving that he was the type of man she disliked: arrogant and presumptuous.

"It was taken out of context."

"Was it? How could your being disparaging about people you did not know be out of context?" she demanded.

Richard paused, eyes flashing at her. "You, of all people, are accusing me of this?"

"Yes, I am." Suddenly feeling uncomfortably wary, Amelia gripped her blanket.

It was his turn to laugh bitterly. "You, a paragon of virtue, who was threatening to knock my quizzing glass out of my hand and stamp on it, if I remember correctly. Yet you were unaware whether I used that same quizzing glass for effect or because there is a fault with my eyesight. Can you not be accused of being as equally disparaging?"

Amelia had flushed deep red at his words. "You heard my silliness?" she whispered in mortification.

"Yes, as did my valet. Very sobering to know that you are being laughed at and presumptions are being made before you have even been seen, as it is now clear that our paths never crossed prior to meeting at my aunt's party." Richard was angry, with her, with himself. He could see her discomfort and was furious that though she deserved to be uncomfortable, he wanted to beg her for forgiveness for being a brute, to bring a smile to her face instead of the look of shame she wore.

"I was wrong to say those words, and the fact that I was being silly in front of my friends is no excuse. You are right. I cannot condemn you when I am at fault of offending in the same way. Please accept my apologies."

"Thank you. I take my leave of you, Miss Beckett. I think we both need to reconsider how we view people we do not know. I hope you are feeling better soon." Richard bowed and stepped away from the doorway he had not left, pulling the door closed behind him.

Briefly closing his eyes, he headed back downstairs and to the library. He was in need of a strong drink to try to forget the look on

Amelia's face. He had never wanted to comfort someone so much and yet escape from her at the same time.

Pouring a large measure the moment he reached the always-full decanter, he emptied the glass and refilled it. What was happening to him?

He was dreaming of the blasted woman, thinking of her when he was awake, and now that he had seen her tousled and undressed, the dreams would most certainly become more vivid.

Pausing the second glass of brandy halfway to his lips, he was struck by a thought; he had not thought of Bea in a while. He had not dreamed of her, the persistent dream of standing at the altar waiting for her. He had not caught himself comparing anyone to her, nor had he needed to say her name aloud, as if stopping would make his feelings disappear.

Instead, his mind had been full of the woman who had the audacity to accuse him of disparaging strangers when she had done the same. A smile touched his lips; he had felt a little guilty at pretending that he might need his quizzing glass to aid his sight. Her stricken look had almost been his undoing, but he had resisted the urge to tell her the truth, that he was a coxcomb who used it for effect. If she had been thinking clearly, she would have no doubt accused him of exactly that, and when she found out that he had been toying with her, he would likely get another roasting.

He could not wait.

Chapter Eight

THE DANCE WENT ahead after the supper as planned. It had been a quiet day. The only thing of note to happen was when Mrs. Evans caused a disturbance at the dining room table by scattering her cutlery everywhere. It had caused a few chuckles, but everyone had soon returned to their plates and hurried to finish their meal. The promise of dancing was not to be underestimated by those who had thought the house party was to be a highlight of the end of the Season and had been sadly disappointed. Amelia offered to play the piano forte. As she had confessed to Richard, her talent was not as excellent as others in the party, but it was good enough to provide accompaniment for the dancers.

Albert and Freddie had taken to heart what Richard had said and entered into the evening in good spirits, dancing every dance with one or other of the ladies. Claude ignored Patricia and Isabelle to dance with the younger ladies, and Richard, under sufferance, danced with whoever did not have a partner. It meant that all the ladies who wished to dance never sat down, and it was the most convivial evening since the start of the house party.

When Amelia's fingers were aching with so much unused exercise, she begged for a respite. Isabelle took her place, and Amelia flopped next to Patricia while the next dance was decided on.

"It has been a good night," Patricia said. "Thank you for sacrificing yourself."

"It isn't really a sacrifice when I would not have been able to dance whether I was playing or not," Amelia said, but there was no bitterness in her tone.

"Is the pain still bad?"

"Not so much, more a throb, just to remind me not to move too fast."

"I wish there was a solution for you."

"There is, rest. I refuse to repine over something I cannot change. Have you seen that Mr. Greenwood is dancing with Mrs. Evans for the second time tonight?" Amelia lowered her voice as the dancers stood in line.

"I wonder which one of her daughters' virtues she is extolling to him?"

"Do you not think that there is a certain connection between the two?" Amelia continued.

"He certainly speaks to her a lot, but she must be old enough to be his mother!" Patricia whispered, shocked.

Amelia laughed. "Hardly! She is older, yes, but it cannot be more than ten years between them."

Patricia looked horrified. "He cannot be seriously considering... No, you think he is considering marrying her?"

Amelia grinned. "Oh, I never said anything about marriage. She is a widow, after all."

"You have been far too influenced by your brother; you are trying to shock me."

"And it seems to be working. Please don't throw daggers at me. I am teasing, sort of. He would not be the first to have a dalliance with a widow, and he is rich, so I can see why she would be attracted to him."

"I can't!"

Amelia burst out laughing at the revulsion in Patricia's voice, which drew the attention of those nearest to them. Shaking her head at her friend, Amelia chuckled. "Do not hold back with your opinions,

Patricia."

Smiling at being teased, Patricia shrugged. "No amount of money…"

"Not for me either, but we are not a widow with two unmarried daughters."

"Oh, to be reliant on that type of lifestyle. I hope none of us is ever that desperate. Though I see from her expression, Mrs. Greenwood has noticed there might be something between the pair."

They both looked over to where Marie sat next to Enid, glowering at her son and Mrs. Evans, who were oblivious to the stares they were attracting.

"He is doing it to torment you," Enid said to her friend.

"It is working," Marie responded. "Why can't the boy do something sensible for once in his life?"

"Because he takes pleasure out of annoying you, just as you enjoy holding the purse strings over him."

Marie looked at her friend. "You really disapprove of my decisions, do you not?"

"I cannot comment on the way you treat your son; that is your decision and choice, but I do object when it involves the girls under my care."

"I have said I was wrong about that!" Marie grumbled. "I have not mentioned anything since, nor tried to change either of their minds."

"Take my advice, do not interfere with whatever he is doing, or intending to do, with Mrs. Evans. It could be harmless. He could just be acting like a mooncalf over her to torment you, but if you try to interfere, you could force him to act in a way he was not intending."

"In other words, let him waste a perfectly good opportunity to secure himself a wife?"

"He might be planning to marry one of her daughters and looking to insinuate himself with her."

"And I might be the Queen of Sheba," Marie muttered to Enid's laugh.

"Your Majesty." Enid bowed her head.

"Oh shut up. I will try and hold my tongue."

"There is a first time for everything. I think you will benefit on this occasion if you do."

"If I were the sensitive sort, I would think you positively disliked me."

"It is because I like you so much that I am brutally honest with you. I would hate to see you unhappy, my friend."

"Umpf," Marie muttered.

They were interrupted from saying more by Freddie's call for there to be a waltz as the final dance. He was well in his cups, cheeks flushed and very jolly. "Miss Sarah wishes it, and so we must!"

Sarah had blushed at everyone looking at her, but she was staring at Freddie as if he was some sort of hero. Everyone turned to Marie to see if she would give permission for the dance to take place.

"Oh go on, it is only another dance, after all." Marie waved her hand at the group.

Freddie cheered at the words and twirled Sarah around until she was in position. Claude asked the elder Miss Evans, though he shot a longing look towards Mrs. Evans. Richard had been talking to one of the fathers who had remained at the party with his wife and daughter, but at the announcement, he crossed to where Amelia and Patricia sat.

"Miss Beckett, could I have this dance?" he asked with a bow.

Amelia looked at him in surprise. "I am not able to dance."

"I thought the waltz might be achievable; it is slower than the other dances, and you have sat so long this evening, you must be wishing to move. We can go at whatever pace you set." Richard could sense that she was torn, but he knew her well enough to know that the evening would have been tedious for her in the extreme and wanted to relieve some of her boredom. It had nothing to do with the fact that he would be holding her in his arms for however long she was able to stand. Perhaps there was a little of that, but overall, his motives were for her comfort and enjoyment to be improved.

"Go on, Amelia. It will do you good; you know how your legs stiffen if you are stationary for too long," Patricia urged, smiling innocently at the glare Amelia aimed in her direction.

"Of course, my lord. This wallflower would be utterly grateful for your condescension," Amelia said, accepting Richard's arm.

"Amelia!" Patricia choked, but Richard just smiled.

"Thank you, Miss Beckett. I know the thought of being civil to me will be nothing more than some sort of penance for you."

"Yes, I am glad you understand my feelings," Amelia responded. Her eyes flew to his face when his hand touched her waist as they moved into position for the dance. It felt intimate, and she should dislike it, but she had to stop the shiver of pleasure as she responded to his touch. Silently cursing how much she enjoyed being so close to him, she was frustrated that both her mind and body were working against her.

Richard had purposely kept more to the side of the room so that their slow progress would not interfere with any of the other dancers. He had stayed away from Amelia all night. Oh, he had seen the dark looks she had sent his way, but he had also seen her look at him sometimes with an almost thoughtful expression. He could have been mistaken, and she could have been concentrating on her music and he had presumed too much, but he trusted his instinct, which told him that she was not as immune to him as she thought.

They moved slowly; it was more of a sway or a shuffle than a dance, and at one point when Amelia caught his foot, she grimaced. "This is foolhardy."

"Are you hurt?"

"No, but this is not dancing in any sense of the word."

"Oh, I do not know. Have you watched my stilted movements all night?"

"If I said yes, that would imply that you were interesting enough to watch," Amelia retorted. Her insides lifted with the flutterings in her stomach when Richard smiled down at her, his blue eyes warming.

"Am I not?"

"As if I would admit to something that would only pander to your overinflated sense of worth."

"I hope such strong feelings are not because I am afflicted with poor eyesight."

Amelia made the mistake of looking once more into his eyes, and seeing laughter and teasing there, she could not stop the smile from her own lips. "You rogue, there is nothing wrong with your eyes."

"I have always thought they are one of my finest features."

"Are you sure you do not aspire to be a fop?"

"I shudder at the thought."

"I remain unconvinced."

"Then it will be my challenge to prove to you just what a fine, perfect specimen I am." Richard was by now loving every minute of holding, teasing, and making her smile.

"One who dislikes wallflowers." Amelia reminded him that he was not completely forgiven.

"That was the opinion of a fool. I am the new and improved version you see before you."

"I am glad you did not mention perfect."

"Ouch, Miss Beckett. What will it cost me to earn your forgiveness?" Richard hoped the dance would go on for hours.

"I am partial to bonbons."

"Ah, did you know I was especially fond of rotund wallflowers?"

Amelia chuckled. "You really are a brute, and I refuse to forgive you."

"I am sorry for what I said." Richard was serious, needing her to know he had been a fool and regretted it.

"I believe you. It just frustrates me that so many suppositions are made when using the derogatory term. Some of us are happy with our lives."

"I do not believe that," Richard said. The dance came to an end at the worst possible moment.

"There is nothing I can do to convince you otherwise," Amelia said stiffly. She curtsied and moved to step away, but Richard offered his arm.

"Please allow me to assist you. We have been standing for some time."

"I notice you did not say I was dancing."

"Perhaps swaying is a better term than standing?"

"Perhaps," Amelia said, sitting once more. "Thank you, my lord."

"Miss Beckett, the pleasure was all mine." Richard bowed and walked away, already missing the touch of her and the way she made him smile. He could not ever remember smiling as much as he had since meeting her.

It was a good thing the end of the party was in sight, or he might be in serious trouble. Thankfully, once she had left his aunt's home, he could return to life as it had been. There was safety in guarding his heart; he was better living that way.

He hoped.

Chapter Nine

THE MORNING AFTER the dance, the quiet was shattered by Mrs. Evans screaming and shouting in the most agitated fashion. Though dressed, Amelia, Patricia and Isabelle were still finishing their hair but left their chamber to see what was happening that had caused so much distress.

"Do not lie to me! You are the only one who could have taken it! I demand you be searched!" Mrs. Evans was screeching at a housemaid who was cowering before her.

"What the devil is going on?" Marie demanded, leaving her own chamber, still in her dressing gown.

"This—this—thief you have employed has stolen my purse! It is all the money I have to last me the quarter, and it is gone!" Mrs. Evans wailed.

The maid turned frightened eyes to her mistress, tears pouring down her face. "I haven't, Missus. I swear on my ma's life that I haven't touched a thing."

"You were lurking in my chamber!" Mrs. Evans spat at her. "I want you searched!"

Holding her arms out to the sides, the maid looked at Marie in appeal. "Please search me. I promise I would never steal from anyone."

"Of course you would not. This is preposterous! Jones, check Gracie's pockets," she said to her butler before turning to Mrs. Evans.

"I am allowing her to be searched in the hope it shuts your screeching up. That girl has never stolen a crumb in her life, and I dislike you accusing my staff of dishonesty."

Mrs. Evans raised herself to her full height. "Are you saying I have made the story up? That I am the one who is lying?"

"I am presuming that you have misplaced your purse. Your room can be turned inside out to try and find it, but for goodness' sake, woman, lower your voice!"

Mrs. Evans looked fit to burst, but flounced back into her room. Claude glared at his mother. "A word, please, Mother."

Marie sighed. "As you wish. Let me return to my chamber; this is far too much noise for so early in the morning."

"Madam, Gracie has no purse or money on her person," Jones said.

"Of course she hasn't," Marie said, nodding at the young girl, who still had tears pouring down her face. "Go and ask Cook for a treat, Gracie. Jones, let her have the morning off and allocate her new duties which keep her away from the Evans women." The final command was said with a look of disgust towards the two Misses Evans. They had been standing at the door of their own chamber, watching everything with flushed cheeks and mortification.

"Could you also keep an eye out for my blue snuffbox? The one with the pattern on top?" Freddie asked the butler. "I seem to have misplaced it."

"Grace does not clean your room," Jones said stiffly.

"Oh no, no! I did not think anything of the sort; it is probably my own doing. I am always leaving the blasted things around," Freddie said quickly. "I just thought if there was a search for a purse, it might be found at the same time."

"Of course, sir," Jones responded.

"I will leave this situation in your hands, Jones, but any trouble, come straight to me," Marie instructed.

She returned to her chamber, followed closely by Claude, who slammed the door to her room. Raised voices were immediately heard, though the words could not be made out.

Everyone moved away, and when Amelia turned, she spotted Richard, who had been standing at the back of the group. He looked as if he was pondering something, but then he looked at Amelia, and she caught her breath. The way his eyes raked over her almost devoured her as he took in her hair, which tumbled down to her waist. He had seen her in her chamber when ill and she had been covered with blankets, but though she was now dressed, she felt suddenly exposed to him. Turning away, she entered her chamber and let out a sigh. He could reduce her to being unable to think or speak with just one look? She was in deep trouble.

Pushing away, or trying to at least, any thoughts of the look in Richard's eyes, she mulled over what had happened. Frowning as Patricia fixed her hair, her friend laughed at her.

"You could at least pretend to be happy with what I am doing with your locks," Patricia said, pulling a strand to get Amelia's attention.

"Ow! Leave some of it in!" Amelia responded. "I was just thinking."

"You surprise me."

"Fine! Do you not think that something is amiss here?"

"That this is a strange house? Yes, I certainly do," Patricia replied.

"Me too," Isabelle said, crossing the room and plonking herself on the chair next to Amelia. "What do you mean specifically?"

"Think back since we arrived here," Amelia started. "I do not know if it was happening before this gathering, but I noticed that items were being moved."

"Moved?"

"As in disappeared."

"Maids do move things around," Patricia said. "It could even be on the command of Mrs. Greenwood."

"No, I am sure that is not it," Amelia persisted. "Mrs. Greenwood likes things just so. I noticed that the moment I walked into the house, and the garden is the same. Everything is symmetrical, perfectly matched and carefully thought out. The first thing I noticed missing was a silver candlestick on the mantelpiece in the music room."

"It is no surprise that candlesticks are moved," Patricia interrupted.

"But why has it never returned?" Amelia demanded. "There was a row of vases on the windowsill at the half landing, but two are no longer there."

"I do not know whether to be worried that there could be a thief amongst us or that you have actually noticed these inconsequential ornaments are missing!" Patricia exclaimed.

Shaking her head at her friend, Amelia turned to Isabelle. "Has your bracelet ever been found?"

"No, it has not, and I have searched and searched, even asking the maids to look for it."

"Yet it was there before we had the stream of visitors," Amelia said smugly.

"That does not prove that it wasn't a maid," Isabelle said. "Though Mrs. Greenwood was convinced Gracie had not taken anything."

"She would have gone against Mrs. Evans just for the spite of it. You can see she dislikes how much time her son is spending with her," Patricia said.

"I remember seeing the snuffbox; it looked very expensive," Isabelle said.

"There does seem to be a number of items unaccounted for," Patricia said.

"True. I think we have a thief in our midst, and I think I know who it is," Amelia said.

"Who?"

"Mr. Greenwood, of course!"

"You cannot be serious?" Isabelle asked.

"Of course I am! Remember what he said when I overheard him?

Something about he was going to take what was his," Amelia explained.

"But stealing from his mother and her guests?" Patricia moved to face Amelia. "Surely that thought is bordering on the ridiculous?"

"Maybe, but there is something havey-cavey going on, and I think we should try to find out what it is," Amelia said.

"I think we would be better served locking our door and being careful with our possessions. If Mrs. Greenwood thought we suspected her son, she would likely throw us out!"

"Perhaps, but I think we have a duty to every maid who is in danger of being accused to find out what is really going on," Amelia insisted.

"I think if we watch everyone carefully, we should be able to work out who the thief is, and then we can try and prove it beyond doubt. We cannot just assume it is Mr. Greenwood because of one comment he made to his mother in the heat of an argument," Patricia said.

"We cannot search his room then?" Amelia asked in mock innocence.

Isabelle and Patricia laughed. "No! We are to be refined young women who would not consider such outrageous action."

"That is so tedious," Amelia moaned, but she dropped the subject. She had not expected her friends to support her in searching a bedchamber, for it was a foolish scheme, but when she was on the landing later that afternoon, walking slowly with her walking sticks, she paused at Claude's chamber.

Mulling over whether it would do any harm to just have a quick peek in the room, she was startled out of her reverie by footsteps behind her. Turning slightly, she was relieved that it wasn't Claude, but could have groaned to see the suspicious expression on Richard's face as he approached her.

"Miss Beckett." He nodded in greeting.

"My lord," Amelia responded.

"Are you in need of assistance?"

"No. Thank you."

The silence between them stretched. Richard rocked back on his heels, hands behind his back, before sighing as if being forced to speak. "Why are you loitering outside my cousin's chamber?"

"I would hardly say walking slowly is loitering!" Amelia responded, tone tart.

"Yet we have been standing here for a few moments now, and you have not taken a step."

"I thought we were having a conversation. It would be rude of me to walk away."

Richard briefly raised his eyes to the heavens. "Come now, Miss Beckett, do not take me for a fool. What is the fascination with Claude's chamber?"

Sighing, Amelia leaned against the wall for support. Standing for any length of time was still difficult, but she would not admit to feeling discomfort. When she confessed the truth of her dallying, she was sure there would be more of a response than simple raised eyes.

"I think Mr. Greenwood is the one who is stealing items," she rushed out. "Go on, tell me you think me an imbecile."

Richard looked taken aback by her words. "Why would I question your sanity over such a thing? You must have thought about it carefully. What is your reasoning?"

The surge of feeling that flooded through Amelia at not being utterly ridiculed by Richard almost made her speechless, but she tried to sound eloquent as she repeated what she had explained to her friends.

"I have noticed that there are items missing about the house, and servants have been searching for lost articles," Richard admitted.

"Really? How many? Not that I am overjoyed that your aunt's possessions are disappearing, but it gives my outrageous theory some merit."

"Are you sure of what you heard?"

"As it involved either myself or one of my friends, I am ashamed to admit that I did eavesdrop and heard him say that he was going to take what was rightfully his."

"That doesn't explain why he would steal from Miss Carrington or Mrs. Evans, and though I dislike the man, I cannot in all conscience see him stealing from his friend. That would be foolish in the extreme," Richard mused.

"True, but can you think what else he meant by his words?"

"With Claude, heaven only knows." Amelia laughed at the statement, but Richard raised his eyebrows at her. "I now understand your suspicion, but it still does not explain why you were hovering here."

Amelia flushed. "You know full well what I was intending to do."

"I was hoping that by being in my company, it might have dissuaded you."

"Have you got a better plan?"

"Than rummaging through my cousin's bedchamber? No. I cannot say that I have an alternative, but that does not make your plan any wiser."

"Go away then, and no one will know," Amelia hissed at him. "You are wasting my time."

"And what if Claude returns to his room?"

"Then I will hide."

"Because you can move so stealthily?"

Richard's tone was mocking, and it made Amelia's teeth grind. No longer filling her with warmth, she had decided he was as annoying as his cousin. "Oh go away! Curse you!"

Shaking his head, Richard stepped forward. "I think I must be the imbecile, Miss Beckett. You have five minutes. I will stand guard at the doorway. And you can take that smile off your face; I am doing this to prevent any accusations of theft from being aimed in your direction. Consider it looking after someone who should know better."

"It would be quicker if you joined me." Amelia scowled at his condemnation, though she knew he was correct.

"As delightful as that sounds, I think not." Richard took his watch out of his waistcoat pocket and, glancing at it, he nodded to her. "Five minutes. No more."

Amelia opened the door, and at there being no sign of Claude's valet, she entered the room as fast as her legs would allow. Looking at the large room, she wondered where to start. There was a desk, wardrobe, and chest of drawers where items could be hidden. Changing her mind about approaching the desk first, she hobbled over to the chest of drawers near the window.

Resting her walking sticks against the wall, she carefully opened the drawers slowly so that if the valet was in the next room, he would not hear her. Grimacing when she saw the first drawer filled with Claude's undergarments, she cringed as she forced herself to move the clothing to feel if there were any of the missing objects in there. Shaking her hand when she had finished, as if it was contaminated in some way, she pushed the drawer closed and opened the next one. Breathing a sigh of relief as cravats filled this one, she moved the pristine cloths to check underneath, but there was nothing to find.

"Miss Beckett!" Richard hissed from the doorway. "I can hear Claude!"

Amelia turned quickly and knocked her walking sticks to the floor. Bending to reach for them, they were whisked out of her grasp as she was half-carried to stand behind the curtains nearest the chest of drawers.

Richard held her sticks, his other arm around Amelia's middle, and pulling her towards him, he shook his head at her, silently demanding that she not speak.

Claude soon entered the room, and instinctively Amelia pressed herself further against Richard, trying to keep herself from the curtain edge. She heard Richard's sharp intake of breath at her movement, but glared at him to remain silent.

"Wilson! I need to change! I am getting out of here. I cannot stand it a moment longer."

"Yes, sir," Wilson replied, making both Richard and Amelia take in the fact that the valet had been very close by. They shared a wide-eyed look, but remained still, though both were struggling with the sensations caused by being in such close proximity to each other.

There were clear sounds of undressing and dressing taking place, and all the time, Claude was muttering to his valet.

"I am sick and tired of being treated like a child," he ranted. "No matter what I do, it is never good enough for her; instead, she extols the virtues of my blasted cousin. If only I could be more like him! Pah! I would rather be a pauper than be Richard. His lofty ways when he doesn't acknowledge what I did for him. I accepted him into my home when he was foisted on me; that was Mother arranging things as always. How did they think I would feel being pushed aside while Mother pandered after Richard all the time and then started singing his praises to me? I have never been considered in any decision she has made."

"I know, sir," the valet murmured as he dressed Claude.

"I tell you, I am not about to marry the wench Mother has chosen for me, no matter how much she threatens to cut me off. I want a real woman, and I intend getting my own way. If I am to marry, it is on my terms. I am certainly not doing what my mother dictates. Blast her to the devil, she promised a house party full of young, attractive women, and there is only one good one between them all. Freddie and Albert are spending more time at the inn than they are here. My reputation will be ruined after this."

"Anyone who knows you, knows your true worth," Wilson soothed.

"I damn well hope so because when I get my inheritance, I will be richer than most of the *ton,* and they had better start showing me some respect."

"I am sure they will."

"Where is my cane? The one with the diamond in the top. There. Good. I will not be returning early, but you will need to wait up," Claude said.

"Yes, sir." Wilson sounded deflated at the command for him to stay awake until all hours.

When Claude had left the room, Wilson gathered up the discarded clothing before leaving through the dressing room door and closing it behind him.

Amelia and Richard remained in place for a few moments in case Claude or Wilson returned, and only when the silence continued did they risk looking at each other.

"That was far too close for comfort," Richard said, letting out a breath, but his arm remained wrapped around Amelia.

"I should not have suggested carrying out a search."

"At last, she sees sense," came the dry response.

Amelia lifted her hand and hit Richard on the shoulder. "There is no need to agree with me."

Richard laughed, but then looked at Amelia. "Miss Beckett, I am astounded to be uttering the words, but I have enjoyed hiding in my cousin's chamber with you. You appear to be a very bad influence on me."

"It can only help expand your reputation. You will be joining Jacob on one of his escapades yet."

"I would much prefer to be with you than your brother."

"That sounds like a compliment; you had better watch yourself or you will get carried away."

"It most certainly is a sincere compliment, and would you mind very much if I got carried away?" He leaned forward and touched his forehead to hers. "Miss Beckett, if you do not move this instant, I am afraid I am going to be unable to stop myself from stealing a kiss."

"Oh," Amelia said; her pupils dilated as her breath tickled his lips. He knew she was not going to pull away from him and rejoiced that she felt warm and safe in his arms. He had wanted to kiss and be kissed by her for too long. "I do not intend to move." Those words were like music to his ears; she was giving him permission, welcoming him, and he was determined to be worthy of her trust.

"That is good to hear," Richard groaned before touching his lips to hers. The first touch was tentative, as if he was still giving her the opportunity to pull away if she should change her mind. Instead, Amelia slid her arms across his chest and around his neck, bringing her even closer and causing Richard to deepen the kiss.

The fragrance of jasmine seemed to surround him as he enjoyed exploring her, touching her hair and tugging at the clips, some of which clattered to the floor. Feeling the thickness of her curls slide through his fingers made him groan with pleasure. It was even more luxurious than he had imagined, and he had a vivid imagination where Miss Amelia Beckett was concerned.

When she sighed into him, he left her lips to kiss along her jawline, loving the way her head fell back, allowing him easy access to her neck. Feeling encumbered by the walking canes, he let them lean against the window, wrapping his now free arm around her and letting his hand roam across her back. Ignoring the clatter of the sticks as they slid ungracefully to the wooden floor, he also at first ignored the cough that he heard.

When a second, louder cough sounded, Richard was finally brought to his senses, and head snapping up, he cursed his weakness for acting on his desires when faced with his cousin's gleeful face.

"Well, well, well, in my chamber, compromising the one I was supposed to marry. Hasn't this turned out to be the most interesting day?"

Chapter Ten

"Did you come looking for me, Miss Beckett? I am sorry if you did and found my cousin instead, though it seems he was trying his hardest to entertain you," Claude said.

"Claude, I am warning you, shut up." Richard growled at his cousin, but kept Amelia in his arms. She had tried to pull away from him when they became aware of Claude, and he did not want her to stumble, but mostly he wanted to protect her, to only let her go when he had made this situation better. How he would do that, he had no idea, but it was his overriding feeling to make everything well. That and he had just experienced a kiss that had turned his world upside down. But instead of being allowed to think about it, to even think about anything, he was now faced with Claude, who would use the situation to his full advantage, if previous experience was anything to go by.

Claude laughed. "Oh no, cousin! This is priceless; you have compromised a woman in my chamber, and you expect me to remain silent on the subject? You must have windmills in your attic if you think I will not fully take advantage of this. How fortunate that I noticed one of my gloves had a smudge of dirt on it before I left the house. From now on, those will be considered my lucky gloves."

"We were looking for something," Amelia said.

"Oh really? That sounds even more intriguing. What did you expect to find behind a curtain and wrapped in an embrace? Oh, silly me, you found yourself a husband!"

"You are being ridiculous. Turn around and leave us be," Richard said.

The words just made Claude laugh even louder, making Amelia wince and turn her head into Richard's frock coat.

"I shall wish you both happy with complete sincerity. You have done me the best of services, cousin, for Mother would never have me marry a woman who has been compromised. Her standards are thankfully high. But with regards to you, it is time you were wed, and at least with this doxy, she cannot run away as the last one did."

Claude did not get another opportunity to speak as Richard moved Amelia swiftly to the side, so she could lean against the wall; Richard then punched Claude on his jaw, sending him sprawling into the room.

"You have gone too far yet again," Richard ground out. "I could kill you for that."

Spitting blood onto the floor, Claude sneered at Richard. "Instead, you will be leg-shackled while still pining after the woman who did not love you enough, just like everyone else in your life. The knowledge of you slowly being tortured will make any beating you give out more than worthwhile. I cannot wait to stand by and watch when you see Bea with your wife on your arm. I expect your wife will soon become accustomed to being second in line after Bea. I almost feel sorry for her, but not quite."

Richard moved and stood over his cousin, but Amelia spoke up before he had time to act.

"Stop!"

Richard turned to her, noticing and faltering at her look of horror.

"I am not marrying anyone."

"You do not have a choice," Claude said, still on the floor.

Amelia was panicking at the situation, but neither man would understand the real reason for her distress. "I am not marrying you, my lord, whether or not you are in love with someone else." She looked at Richard, anguish in her eyes. "I am sorry. I should not have involved you in my foolish scheme." Hobbling out of the room, she did not turn around but disappeared as fast as she could muster.

Claude slid away from Richard, but remained on the floor. He was not willing to stand in case Richard took another lunge at him, but Amelia's actions had affected Richard, which Claude was keen to point out. "The situation becomes more interesting by the minute. Did she really come in here looking for me, and you accosted her?"

"Do not be ridiculous."

"Says the one found kissing a guest in my chamber. Why were you in here? You must agree that it is an odd place for an illicit meeting."

"We were looking for the missing items." Richard hated to admit the real reason for their presence in Claude's room, but a small part of him hoped that Claude would be diverted from his determination to cause a scandal.

"What missing items? I have not lost anything." Claude was clearly confused.

Sighing at the fact that Claude was being genuine in his puzzlement, Richard continued. "There are items that have gone missing in the house. We were trying to find them."

Claude's eyes narrowed. "You thought I took Mrs. Evans's purse?"

"No. Maybe. I haven't got a clue; it was a foolish thought."

Claude sat up straighter. "You think I am a thief? I always knew you were jealous of me, but this is beyond belief! You must be insane!"

"You want what is yours." Richard shrugged, trying to hide his embarrassment, for he certainly felt out of sorts after what he had shared with Amelia, and even worse, now he was at an even bigger disadvantage with Claude.

"And I am going to get it, but that does not involve stealing from a widow and the only person who has shown me any respect and consideration during her stay."

"Your mother will never accept a marriage between you," Richard warned.

"Mother can mind her own business," Claude snapped. "And so can you. I am determined to live my life the way I want to. You, on the other hand, have more pressing matters to deal with. Are you not going to chase the chit and try to convince her that the only option she has of remaining in decent society is to marry you? For I will be passing on my congratulations this evening at dinner."

"I always knew you were a worthless human being, but you really are the worst kind of bully, aren't you? You are going to end your life lonely and friendless if you do not change." Richard did not wait for a response before leaving his cousin's chamber.

"But I will not be the only one suffering, dear cousin," Claude muttered, finally standing up and moving to his desk.

AMELIA CLOSED THE door of her chamber, surprised to find Patricia already inside. Leaning against the door, she closed her eyes, hoping the solidity of the wood would calm her as she tried to stem the panic rising in her chest and the tears stinging behind her eyelids.

"Amelia! What is it?" Patricia asked, immediately by Amelia's side.

"I cannot marry him. I cannot marry anyone, but especially him."

"Mr. Greenwood? I thought Mrs. Greenwood had accepted your refusal. What has she done?"

"No. The earl," Amelia said, tears leaking onto her cheeks.

"Oh, Amelia, what has happened?" Patricia asked. "Come, sit and tell me everything."

Amelia accepted Patricia's arm until she was seated on the stool in front of the dressing table. Wiping her eyes, she smiled tearfully at her friend. "I have been really stupid."

"Tell me what has upset you so much," Patricia soothed.

Recounting what had happened until she had left Claude's chamber, Amelia finished with a sob. "Even if he were to ask me to marry him, I cannot."

"I know you did not set out for anything to happen between you, but surely the fact that you kissed must mean there is some attraction there? We have teased you about how often he looks at you, and he is always eager to seek you out to speak with. Perhaps he has feelings that he has not yet confessed."

"A kiss is not a declaration of wishing to marry."

"No, but it is certainly a start, and I am afraid to point out that with Mr. Greenwood discovering you…"

"It was the most wonderful kiss I could possibly imagine." Amelia allowed herself to enjoy the memory of being held and feeling wrapped in strong arms while being tenderly yet passionately worshipped.

"Then why is the thought of marrying him so repulsive?"

"Because of *these*!" Amelia slapped her legs.

"Oh Amelia, no," Patricia said.

"How can I marry anyone, but especially one who already thought I was pitiable? If we married, I could not stand to see the revulsion on his face when he saw me undressed. Since the accident, I have accepted that I could never be seen by a husband, and I had become accustomed to it, I really had, and then he had to kiss me and make me want things I can never have!"

"If he loved you, it would not matter," Patricia said.

"He might have kissed me, but he is in love with another."

"How do you know that?"

"From the way he reacted when Mr. Greenwood taunted him about it, and his aunt mentioned her at lunch the other day. Someone named Bea deserted him, but he still follows her around. That does not sound like a man ready to propose to another, does it?"

"But you have been found in a compromising position. If Mr.

Greenwood lets it be known..." Patricia did not need to finish the sentence; they both knew the outcome of Claude making his discovery public.

"I know that I will be ruined, but I cannot think straight. Marrying cannot be the only option we have, the earl clearly does not wish to marry me, and I cannot marry him. Please forgive my cowardice, but I cannot face them at the dining table this evening; I need to prepare to leave."

"Amelia, you cannot run away from this."

"I know, and as Mr. Greenwood pointed out, I brought about my own downfall, which I am fully aware of. I just need this evening to think."

"I can understand that, and I will make your excuses, but I think you should seriously consider marrying his lordship."

"Let us not forget that he has not actually offered for me," Amelia said dryly.

"But he must!" Patricia responded.

"I hope he does not, then that will be one less difficult conversation I will need to have."

"I will go and seek out Isabelle and let her know what is happening. At least everyone will accept our excuse of you being too tired to come down to dinner, but I also think I should tell Grandmother about what has happened."

"Not yet. Tell her soon, but not this evening," Amelia pleaded.

"Fine, but I am doing this under protest," Patricia said, kissing Amelia's cheek. "I will find Isabelle and then inform the housekeeper that you need a tray. Try not to worry."

"Thank you, you are the best of friends."

When Patricia had left the room, Amelia put her arms on the dressing table and rested her head on them. She could not face being married and seeing the pity or disgust on her husband's face as he saw the scarring on her legs, but there was a lump of longing in her stomach that would not go away. The kisses they had shared had fanned something which had already been growing almost from the first moment that she saw him. It was a yearning to have what felt like the impossible.

Now they had kissed, and she had experienced just how good being with him could be; that unrequited longing was going to turn into something that ate away at her insides for a long time to come. Allowing the tears to fall, she could see nothing but a solitary future ahead.

∞

THE EVENING MEAL was strained. Richard had never felt so on edge as he did when expecting his cousin to arrive and cause trouble at any moment. Disappointed but not surprised when he heard Amelia was not joining them, he was tense until his aunt acknowledged that Claude would also be missing. At least in that regard he could relax, knowing that Claude would not be making any announcements. Noticing that Albert and Freddie were not impressed at the news Claude was absent, Richard allowed himself to hope his cousin would be diverted enough by the anger of his friends to forget the need to gloat over what had happened. It was a vain hope, but it was the only one he had.

Reluctant to join in any inane conversation, yet again his taciturn reputation came in useful. He spoke to Miss Evans and his aunt, but managed to get through the meal without much effort. As his thoughts were filled with the afternoon's events, it was a good thing.

All he could think about was how good it had felt to have Amelia in his arms, but then his face would cloud over as he remembered that she had looked horrified at the prospect of marrying him. Angry at not being good enough yet again, he consoled himself with the thought that he did not wish to marry, especially a woman who so clearly disliked him.

Frustration pulsed through him just as fast as arousal had when exploring Amelia's mouth, neck, and cheeks. He was astounded to perceive that the thought of marrying her did not make him falter as much as it should. The stab of pain he had felt when looking at her as what Claude was saying sank in, would haunt him and make him curse his own feelings. It seemed that where relationships were concerned, yet again, he was at a disadvantage.

Would he have offered if she had remained in the room? As a gentleman, he should, but that would have made it seem as though he was doing Claude's bidding. Not a good thought, as Claude would never stop crowing about it. Thankfully, with regards to Claude having the upper hand, Amelia had left, but now they needed to speak about what had happened and what they were going to do about it. Not for the first time, he imagined waking up with Amelia wrapped in his embrace, and he silently cursed himself and his need to give love and be loved. He should have learned with Bea; he thought he had, and then Amelia had come along. It was all a blasted mess, and he had no idea how it would be resolved.

Fortunately, he would not have long to wait to find out.

Chapter Eleven

MARIE STORMED INTO the breakfast room and slapped the paper in front of Richard. "What is the meaning of this?"

"Good morning to you too, Aunt," Richard responded, trying to move the newspaper from where it covered his coffee cup.

"Don't you good morning me! How dare you go against my wishes! I was clear from the start with what I wanted to happen! How could you?" Marie ranted.

Enid walked into the room, followed by Patricia, Isabelle, and finally Amelia, who looked uncomfortable when seeing Richard, but continued towards the table nonetheless.

"What is it, Marie?" Enid asked.

"As if you do not already know!" Marie turned to Amelia. "I actually believed you when you said you were not intending marrying; you must have congratulated yourself on so easily fooling an old woman. Did you set out to capture him before you even arrived? Or did you think to make a decision once you were settled in and had seen who else was here? You have certainly done well for yourself. I expect you are pleased as punch."

"I have no idea what you are referring to," Amelia said in complete confusion.

"You might have fooled me once, but you will not do it again," Marie snapped.

Richard gave a cough, focusing everyone's attention away from

Marie's anger. "Miss Beckett, I think you should see this," he said, holding out the folded paper, his hand shaking a little.

Amelia crossed to him and, without meeting his gaze, accepted the paper and started reading. Only the merest of seconds passed before she let out a surprised sound and looked at Richard. "You did this?"

"No. I did not," Richard responded, taking no pleasure in seeing the flush fade from her cheeks as it probably had from his.

"My family!" Amelia moaned, stumbling to the nearest chair and sinking onto it. "What will they think?"

Enid had removed the newspaper from Amelia's grasp, and after reading what had upset her so much, she looked at Richard. "If you did not post this…"

"My cousin must have been the one to send it off."

"What are you saying?" Marie demanded while Patricia and Isabelle read the article. "Give me that! Why would Claude do something like this? It is not worded as if from him. *The Earl of Douglas, Viscount of Edgewear, Mr. Richard Fox, would like to announce his recent marriage to Miss Amelia Beckett. The happy couple are undertaking a wedding trip and will soon be returning to London to celebrate with friends and family.*"

Amelia looked in horror at Patricia. "He has ruined me."

"You need to get a special license," Enid said to Richard. "Amelia, send an express to your parents. The damage can be reduced if you act quickly."

"They will never forgive me," Amelia said.

"Of course they will, especially when you return with your husband," Patricia said, crouching in front of Amelia.

"I cannot…" Amelia started.

"You must," Patricia whispered to her friend while glancing at Richard. "It is the only option you have."

Amelia looked at Richard. He had stood and was motionless, hands behind his back, mouth pinched and frown lines firmly in place. "I am sorry," she said.

"As am I, but the only option we have is to obtain a special license."

"I know," Amelia responded quietly.

"I shall return when I have one." Richard bowed and left the room.

Marie sat across from Amelia. "Claude did this? Why?"

"He caught us kissing," Amelia said, a blush staining her cheeks.

"Then you did set out to catch Richard?"

"No! Not at all! I did not want to marry, and I still don't."

"Marie, you cannot blame Amelia for this situation. You need to speak to Claude," Enid said. "Even if he did catch them, why do something so malicious as to send out a notice to the *Times*?"

"Find my son and say I need to speak to him urgently," Marie commanded one of the footmen who had been in the breakfast room as the scene unfolded. Nodding to his mistress, he left the room and did not return for some time.

No one ate or drank anything while they waited, all appetites gone. Marie commanded the tea to be replenished after waiting for a full ten minutes, but when Jones walked into the room, his face grim, she paused in giving out instructions.

"What is it? Where is Claude?" she demanded of her butler.

"He left the house very early this morning," Jones said. "The stable hands were woken by the carriage leaving at sunrise."

"Devil take him!" Marie ground out. "Just wait until he returns!"

"Mrs. Greenwood, if I could have a private word," Jones said, looking uncomfortable.

"Oh, out with it, man! Everyone knows what Claude is; you might as well speak."

"The safe in the study is open, and Mrs. Evans is also missing," Jones said.

"My safe? Has anything gone?" Marie stood.

"If there was money in there, then yes," Jones said.

Marie seemed to sag. "Have they gone together?"

"It would appear so, but we do not yet know for certain."

"What about the Misses Evans?" Enid asked.

"The maid said they are having hot chocolate in their chamber; they do not yet appear to know that their mother has left."

"What a mess!" Enid said.

"Enid, go and speak to them. I cannot," Marie said. "I need to check what is missing."

Enid nodded and indicated that Patricia should follow her. They left the room, along with the servants and Marie.

Isabelle looked at Amelia. "It will work out, you will see."

Amelia knew there was no point in disagreeing with her friend; she would always try to look at it in the most positive way. No one could understand her fear of being so vulnerable in front of a husband; they did not see what she did every time she undressed. The thought of seeing Richard's repulsion made her feel queasy.

She was only brought out of her reverie by the grim expressions on Enid and Patricia's faces when they returned to the breakfast room a good half hour after they had left. Enid ordered some tea before sitting at the now cleared table.

"That was harder than I expected it to be," she said.

"Did they not know about their mother leaving?" Isabelle asked.

"No, we have left two hysterical young girls," Patricia said. "Thankfully, they have each other, and giving them a little time alone to gather themselves seemed to be the best thing to do."

"I have promised we will support them to return home in any way we can, but to be honest, if their mother is not there, I dread to think what will become of them," Enid said.

"The poor things!" Isabelle said.

"I know, it was heart breaking to see their distress. Grandmamma was far better with them than I could have been," Patricia acknowledged. "This party just gets more complicated by the moment."

"There is no party," Marie said, walking into the room, followed by a footman with a heavily laden tea tray. She looked at the tea things as he placed them on the table. "Go and fetch me some brandy; tea is not going to help in this situation."

"It is barely eleven o'clock," Enid pointed out to her friend.

"After this morning, I do not care what time it is. I have got Jones to tell Claude's friends and the others that the party is over and they are to leave immediately."

"You cannot send the Evans girls away," Enid cautioned.

"And why not?" Marie demanded.

"They knew nothing about what has happened and have been abandoned by their only surviving parent. We cannot in all good conscience let them leave without some form of protection."

"I will not be paying for anything for them. For now, at least, I cannot." Marie looked older than her years, seeming to have aged since she had read the notice in the newspaper. Accepting the decanter of brandy and glass from the footman, she waved him away. "Close the door on your way out," she commanded.

"Is it so bad?" Enid asked her friend.

"Yes. He has taken my jewels, my money, and the deeds to the property. He cannot sell it outright, for some is entailed, but there is land and farms he can sell. He was true to his word in that he was going to take what he could."

"But that is theft!" Patricia exclaimed, unable to hold her tongue. "It is still your property."

"And he knows me well enough to play on the fact that, although I presently despise him, I will not raise a fuss and see him hanged for stealing from his mother. I could not bear the scandal, and my maternal feelings, however limited, would not wish him in that much trouble."

"I am sorry, Marie," Enid said. "If there is anything I can do, you know you only need to ask."

"Thank you. And thank you for not gloating. You have every right to; you warned me about trying to control him too much. I suppose I shall see him next when he has run out of money; only, this time, I will not have the blunt to get him out of trouble, for he knows as well as I do that I cannot access the capital of my funds. Those are tied up until I die; I can only have the interest off it. It seems you chose the right one," she said to Amelia. "Congratulate yourself on having a lucky escape."

Amelia, Patricia, and Isabelle had all been feeling uncomfortable at being present when such personal information was being revealed, but Amelia was annoyed that she was still not believed about not setting out to capture Richard.

"I did not..." she started, but Marie interrupted her.

"It does not matter. What is done cannot be undone at this point, but I do suggest that you send an express to your parents if what you say is true. They will have read the newspapers by now."

"May I be excused?" Amelia asked Enid.

"Yes, and I would start to prepare for when his lordship returns," Enid said gently. "There is no time to lose in arranging matters so they can be settled. The longer you are here unmarried, the more danger there is of scandal, especially with everyone being thrown out of the house." She sent a dry look towards Marie, who just took a large gulp of brandy.

Amelia left the room, not knowing what upset her the most, that she was to be married when she was so imperfect or that she had let her parents and her family down. All she could hope was that this would not impact on her sisters' chances of securing a good match. If they were able to offset the scandal so that it did not affect them, she could rest a little easier at least.

It was a thought that only gave her a modicum of comfort as she slowly walked up the stairs.

Chapter Twelve

RICHARD RETURNED TO the house in the late afternoon. There was a quietness that immediately alerted him to the fact that other things must have happened since he had left to make the arrangements.

Cursing himself that his first panicked thought was that Amelia had left, he entered the drawing room to thankfully find his aunt alone.

"You have returned then. Part of me suspected that you would disappear, but then I remembered that you were the decent one, and it is my damnable son who vanishes after causing trouble," Marie said, her words slurring slightly.

"Aunt, are you unwell?" Richard asked, immediately crossing the room and sitting next to his aunt and taking her hand in his.

"I am in my cups." Marie smiled at him. "I find it deadens the pain a little."

From the look of her, Richard could see she was deeply upset; he had never seen her looking so dejected. "Are you still angry that I am marrying the girl you had chosen for Claude?"

"No. You have probably done her a good turn," Marie said.

"I doubt she is thinking that from the look on her face when I left. A trip to Newgate is probably preferable to being wed to me." There was bitterness in his voice, which he did not bother to hide.

"Then she is a fool, like my son. Claude has gone, taken all the money he could find, jewels, and the deeds," Marie said. "He has not ruined us, but he has certainly taken as much as he could."

"Good God! He accused me of being insane, but I think it is he who has gone mad! What is he thinking?" Richard exclaimed.

"Oh, and to add insult to injury, he has taken the Evans woman with him."

"The fool!" Richard stood and paced the room. "I cannot see him settling with her and her daughters. He must be setting her up as his mistress, but with the daughters? That is very strange indeed."

"They have left the girls here. Unprotected and penniless."

Sinking onto a sofa, Richard was astonished. "How can a mother abandon her girls? She must know that you would not look kindly on them because of her liaison with Claude."

"I admit I wanted to throw them out when I first heard what had happened, but thankfully for them, Enid was here and made me see sense. I have been robbed by my own kin and have two girls to do something with."

"What are you going to do with them? Surely you cannot wish for them to remain here until their mother returns?"

"Would you ever come back if you were their mother?" Marie asked dryly.

"No," Richard answered. "There must be some relative who could take them in, I suppose."

"That is what we have presumed, but Enid suggested we leave them be for now. Apparently, they were quite hysterical when she told them what had happened." Marie noticed the expression on Richard's face. "Are you going all melancholy on me because you feel sympathy for anyone who has been deserted?"

Smiling a little, he nodded. "Probably."

"I take it everything is arranged?"

"Yes, and I have spoken to the clergyman. He will be attending the house at nine in the morning to perform the ceremony," Richard said dully.

"You have to marry her."

"I know. I also know that it is the last thing she wants."

"She kissed you. There are consequences to our actions, and she should have considered them before taking a risk," Marie said.

"It was I who kissed her first," Richard defended.

"That is a surprise. Was it a spur of the moment action, or has Bea lessened her hold over you?"

"I have not thought of Bea, well, only when reminded to do so, for days now." There was no point in hiding anything from his aunt; he had always been honest with her.

Marie smiled. "Then there is something good to come from all of this. I wish you happy, boy, you certainly deserve it more than most, and she will keep you on your toes. I just hope you do not come to regret your actions. I still say you would have been better with a meek wife."

Richard laughed. "Sometimes I truly believe that you do not know me. A meek wife would bore me within a sennight. At least with Miss Beckett, I know life will not be tedious, though I also know there will not be the love I had hoped for when I married."

"If she returned your kisses, she is not immune to you. No woman kisses someone she does not want to."

Richard was not convinced of the truth of his aunt's statement, but despite that, he allowed himself to feel a glimmer of hope. Amelia had moaned with pleasure and responded to him when they had kissed; perhaps she did like him a little. It was something that could give him encouragement.

∞

RICHARD'S MORE BUOYANT thoughts did not survive beyond the following morning. As he watched Amelia enter the drawing room in which the ceremony was to be held, he caught his breath. She looked beautiful in a pale-blue silk gown. It was the finest dress he had seen her in, and it made him appreciate how regal she looked. Her hair was softer, curls falling around her face and onto her neck, and she carried a posy of flowers.

He would have smiled in welcome and held out his hand to her, as she still walked with a little stiffness, but the look in her eyes made him stand stock still. She had clearly been crying, and the thought that it was because she did not wish to marry him tore at his insides. If he could have thought of a way of saving her reputation that did not involve them marrying, he would have stopped proceedings, though that thought did not offer him any comfort.

Her usual smile was gone to be replaced by the most haunted expression he had seen on anyone. His own mouth turned down in response, and holding his hands tightly behind his back, he looked at the clergyman, unable to look at Amelia anymore.

Richard's reaction to her convinced Amelia that she was making the biggest mistake of her life, yet there was nothing she could do about it. She was about to marry a cold, unfeeling man, one who she had mistakenly thought was someone she could love. Failing to see the hurt in Richard's expression, she saw his withdrawal as a wish to be far away from the situation he was being forced into. Tears once more filled her eyes.

The panic threatened to rise again as the clergyman started to speak, and she thought of what marriage would entail, but apart from gripping her hands to try to stop them from shaking, she stood next to Richard and nodded as the clergyman continued the service. She could only guess at what he thought of the situation, and she tried to avoid any eye contact with him. Anticipating seeing disgust from one man was more than enough to deal with.

The service was thankfully short, and the clergyman made his escape as soon as he could. Only Patricia, Isabelle, and Enid had watched the service, two of them acting as witnesses for the register. Marie had chosen to remain in her chamber because of the aftereffects of the brandy, though she had kissed Richard before she had gone to bed and wished him every happiness.

There was to be no wedding breakfast, but Richard had sent a message to his bride before the wedding to say that he would need to go through some details after they had been married. When he asked Amelia to join him in his aunt's study, she nodded meekly and followed him.

Closing the door once they were in the room, they stood facing one another in silence for a moment.

"I hope we can find a way to rub along together," Richard finally said, breaking the tense moment.

"I hope so too, but I cannot… do you expect…?" Amelia stuttered.

"Am I so repulsive?" Richard asked before shaking his head in disgust at himself. "Do not answer that; I do not care what your answer is. I will not be seeking to consummate the marriage, if that is your concern." He felt even more deflated when he heard Amelia's sigh of relief at his words, but he continued. "As my wife, you need to know about my finances and what will be given to you."

"I do not want anything. I will continue to live off my allowance left by my grandmother," Amelia said quickly.

"As my wife, there will be the necessity of attending a certain number of events and entertainments, requiring the height of fashion to be worn. I will accept a lot that I am not happy about, but I refuse to be ridiculed for being a pinchpenny with my wife."

"I see. I beg pardon yet again for my involvement in all of this. I know it is not going to be easy for you."

"No. We were both at fault and are going to suffer because of it," Richard said. He was once more hiding behind the stiffly cold façade. It had helped him through so much that it was natural to revert to it when he was hurting and feeling lost once more. It was the only way he knew to protect himself, but he was no longer sure that it was effective if the lump of lead in his stomach was anything to go by.

Amelia did not answer. Her own feelings were reeling from being with a man who was once more a complete stranger to her. Had she really been wrapped in his arms only a few days ago, feeling as if she could never feel so content in any other situation as she did in those precious moments? Now, it all felt as if that had been a dream, and she was in the middle of a nightmare with no way out.

As Richard explained his financial situation, there was none of the usual teasing between them; Amelia merely nodded when Richard told her how he would arrange things. "As there will be no children, I do not need to arrange provision for them," he said, standing once more. He needed to get out of the room and away from the woman he no longer felt a connection with, but was tied to for the rest of his life.

Amelia's eyes had flown to his eyes at his words, and she had paled further, which was a feat indeed. "I-I suppose so," she whispered.

Richard paused. "I will not acknowledge any children from any dalliance you might have. We have been forced into this situation, but I will not meekly accept another man's bastards."

Amelia winced at the words, but sat up taller. "I would never ask anyone to do such a thing, and I am insulted that you would consider that I would."

"Are you really surprised? I thought I knew you, but you continue to surprise me at every turn. I am being honest about our married life to ensure you understand my feelings on the matter."

"It is not an appealing future at the moment," Amelia snapped, still stinging at the suggestion she would betray him with another.

"Then we are at least in agreement over something," Richard said, leaving the room.

Amelia ground her teeth. "Blast my foolishness!" she cursed herself. "Why did I think I could solve the mystery of the missing items? Amelia, you have excelled yourself this time."

Getting up, she left the room, wondering what the future would hold.

※

RICHARD KNOCKED ON his aunt's chamber door and entered when hearing her call out. "Are you well enough for a visitor?" he asked.

"I am not ill, just a foolish old woman who should not drink brandy," Marie said.

"You are not old." Richard came and sat on the edge of the bed.

"I feel it, and I am certainly foolish. I know just how narrow-minded I have been, and because I would not listen to you, it has cost me everything," Marie said.

"We are both guilty of not listening to the other," Richard said. "I was like some Johnny raw, letting the proximity of a woman turn my head. Look how well that turned out."

"You said that you had stopped thinking of Bea so much; that is some good to come out of all this."

"Yes, I had, and now look at me. Married to a woman who cannot bear to be near me. At least a marriage with Bea would have allowed me to love her."

"She would have destroyed you," Marie said. Taking hold of Richard's hands, she looked him in the eyes. "Give Amelia a chance; something might grow between you. I might have been denying it, but there is definitely a spark between the pair of you."

"Until we married, when she seemed to have had a change of heart," Richard said dryly. "Enough of this melancholy; it was not the reason I came to you. I wanted to know what you intend doing with the Misses Evans."

Marie flopped back onto her pillows. "They have done nothing wrong, but blast it, I want them out of the house."

They were interrupted by Enid's entrance. She was carrying a tea tray, which Richard moved to take from her and set down.

"Have my servants deserted me as well as my son?" Marie asked.

"No. I thought I would save them a task, that is all," Enid said, stirring the tea. "I will leave you in peace when I have poured it."

"There is no need; you might be able to help. Richard was just asking what was going to happen to the Evans girls."

"I can take them back to town. Now that they have stopped crying, they have admitted that there is a grandmother on their father's side who they could appeal to. Apparently, she did not like their mother," Enid said while handing out the tea.

"She is not the only one," Marie muttered.

"Quite. I am happy to return to London with them."

"Could you not stay here?" Marie asked, surprising Richard and Enid with her request.

"Of course, but would it not be best to sort things out with Claude when he returns, just the two of you?" Enid asked.

"I doubt he will return, and I would like your counsel in this mess."

"I can help, Aunt," Richard said quickly.

"No. You are newly married and need to go and visit your bride's parents. You have enough to contend with sorting out that mess which Claude caused. If Enid is willing to stay, she is all I need."

"I am sure Patricia and Isabelle will be happy to stay on with me."

"Thank you," Marie said. "I would appreciate that."

"But that does not solve the problem with the Evanses," Enid said.

"We will take them to London and ensure they arrive at their grandmother's safely," Richard said. "It might help if I am there if she proves to be a difficult character."

"Thank you, that puts my mind at rest and relieves us of that problem at least," Enid said to them both. "When do you intend leaving?"

"We might as well go first thing tomorrow," Richard said, standing. "I will leave you both and tell my *wife* of the plans." Both noticed the disparaging way he used the term wife but did not respond to it.

"I will get out of my bed soon," Marie said. "I hate those who lay around all day repining. I am not usually so weak."

"It has been a shock, Aunt. No one would censure you for taking to your bed." Richard kissed his aunt and left the room.

"I do not know who I feel sorry the most," Enid said when Richard had closed the door behind him. "They both cannot see what is obvious to an onlooker, and each is hurting because of it."

"There is nothing we can do for them. If there is one thing I have learned through all of this, it is that I am not meddling in anyone else's business ever again."

"Now that is something I cannot wait to see." Enid grinned at her friend. "Now, what are we going to do about that son of yours?"

Marie groaned. "I need more brandy!" She pulled the blankets over her head at Enid's laughter.

Chapter Thirteen

THE FOUR SAT in silence as the carriage pulled away from the house. Amelia sat next to Richard, facing the two young girls who looked terrified of him. There was no longer any flirting or trying to score points off any advantage they could as they had previously done. Instead, they looked young, frightened, and upset.

By the time they reached the inn for the night, Amelia had a terrible headache and could honestly say that she had never had a worse journey. The carriage was well sprung and comfortable, but with Richard gazing out of the window for the whole time and only being able to get one-word answers from Sarah and Laura, she was desperate for escape.

The wedding night had been spent in her chamber with Isabelle and Patricia, and she was told in no uncertain terms that she was expected to share a room with Sarah and Laura in order to offer some chaperonage to the girls. That they had been accompanied by Richard's valet and a maid was irrelevant; Amelia had made herself understood when they had spoken before leaving, and Richard was doggedly sticking to her request of there being no contact between them.

Amelia sat on the edge of the bed while the girls settled on two truckle beds that had been set up. She put her head in her hands.

"Lady Douglas, are you unwell?" Laura asked.

"What? Oh no." Amelia smiled a little. "For a moment there, I wondered who Lady Douglas was."

"I suppose it would take some getting used to, but are you sure everything is well? You have only just recovered from your accident, and you seem out of sorts."

"I am a little stiff with not walking much today, but it is nothing a good night's sleep won't cure," Amelia replied.

"I was unfair when I ridiculed you about your injury," Sarah said, her eyes filling with tears. "You have been nothing but kind to us, and I was wicked to say such things."

"Do not worry, it is of no consequence. I am maimed, so you were not saying an untruth," Amelia said, smiling at Sarah.

"It was unforgivable. I could never understand why mother instructed us most insistently that we had to appear to advantage no matter what. I felt awful for the rest of the day after I had spoken so meanly," Sarah explained, wiping her tears away.

"She wanted you to get a husband, but you would always look to best advantage if you had just been yourself."

"The Season is bad enough when you have no dowry and a mother who is very often gauche, but at a house party when everyone is watching you, waiting for you to make a mistake, it was horrible," Laura chimed in, having been silent until this point.

Amelia did not know what to say to Laura's words. It would not help if she agreed, and yet she could not bring herself to defend Mrs. Evans.

"And now that she has caused a scandal, we will never be seen in society again," Sarah sniffed.

"Your grandmother might have different views on that," Amelia soothed.

"I just hope she takes us in; anything else we can but dream of," Laura muttered.

"Try not to worry about that now. We will face whatever we need to when we arrive in London," Amelia said.

"Thank you. We are fully aware that we do not deserve anyone's help, but we are very grateful for it," Laura said.

"My lady, could I have a word, please?" The maid interrupted the conversation.

"Of course, please come in," Amelia said. She did not know the maid, her being one of Mrs. Greenwood's, but she seemed efficient enough.

"I think it would be best if you came into the dressing room," the maid insisted.

Amelia stood up and followed the maid. The room could hardly be considered a dressing room; it was tiny, just enough to fit some of their luggage, a washstand, dressing table, mirror, and a truckle bed for the servant.

"Is there something amiss?" Amelia asked as the maid closed the door.

"There is, my lady. I am sorry to have to raise this now, but when I was getting out the young ladies' nightclothes, I found something you need to see."

"Go ahead," Amelia said with an acute sense of foreboding.

The maid opened the lid of a portmanteau and pulled aside the clothes; there was a large bag, which seemed out of place, crushing the clothes beneath it.

"What is in the bag?" Amelia asked.

"Everything that was taken from Mrs. Greenwood's, except the vases. There is also a note," the maid said, opening the bag to show Amelia the contents.

Only just holding in the groan that she wanted to utter, Amelia moved an item or two, seeing Freddie's snuffbox, Isabelle's bracelet, cutlery, and a small candlestick. There was also a reticule, which, on closer inspection, contained quite a bit of money.

"I am presuming the vases will be secreted somewhere else in their luggage; they were too big to fit in this bag," Amelia said.

"Would you like me to search through everything?"

"Not for now. Leave this with me." Setting her shoulders, she returned to the room, holding the bag.

Laura looked at her with a frown on her face. "What are you doing with Mama's bag?"

"This belongs to your mother?" Amelia asked.

"Yes, she put it in our portmanteau, saying that she had no room in hers," Laura answered.

"Why were you packed up?"

"Mother said we were going to leave, that she had had enough. She had us pack everything two days before she disappeared with Mr. Greenwood," Laura said. She had not stopped staring at the bag, and as she spoke, became paler as some intuition warned her of impending trouble. "Lady Douglas, what is in that bag?"

"You do not know?"

"No."

Amelia walked to the bed and emptied the bag of its contents. Sarah and Laura both reared back when the items clattered onto the covers.

"We-we did not take anything!" Laura stuttered, backing away from the bed. "This is not our doing."

Sarah looked in panic at her sister. "Mama was the thief?" she asked.

"She must have been, and she put everything in our luggage. She even pretended to steal from herself. Look, that is one of her reticules. She has put the blame on us."

"We will hang for stealing!" Sarah wailed before starting to scream out sobs. "I don't want to hang! I just want to go home!"

Amelia tried to calm her, but the young girl was inconsolable with fear. After ten minutes, the door was opened, and Richard marched in.

"What the devil is going on here? You can be heard all the way to the taproom. What in blazes are those?" He pointed at the stolen items.

Amelia moved over to Richard. "It seems Mrs. Evans left her daughters a final going away present."

Richard raised an eyebrow at her words. "That would be a very convenient excuse on being discovered."

"We did not do anything, my lord!" Laura cried, grabbing at Richard's sleeve. "We have never stolen anything, though we have nothing to speak of."

Amelia moved and prised Laura's fingers from Richard's arm, wondering if the fine wool of the frock coat would ever recover from such rough handling. She wrapped her arm around Laura's shoulders and walked her to Sarah. "Nothing is going to happen to you both; no one is going to hang."

"But he does not believe us!" Laura wailed, starting to reach the volume of her sister.

"I believe you, and I give you my word that all will be well," Amelia said firmly. "Now dry your eyes." Knocking on the dressing room door, she indicated the maid should come in. "Miss Evans and Miss Sarah are a little upset. Could you help them wash up and then take them to our private room and order tea and cakes for them? I think they will feel a little better away from these," she said of the items on the bed.

"Yes, my lady," the maid said, and immediately ushered the girls into the dressing room and closed the door firmly behind them.

"You should not have given them such a promise," Richard said.

"Oh come on! They are as much thieves as we are!" Amelia said.

"They could be good actresses."

"No, their upset was genuine. They feel bad enough that Mrs. Evans has abandoned them, now they think she has set them up to be hanged. Have some pity for what they must be feeling."

Richard rubbed his hand over his face. He knew all too well some of what they were feeling, at least. "What a callous woman!"

"We can agree on that, at least," Amelia said, standing over the bed. "I did not look at the paper before now, thinking it was not pertinent to anything, but look, it is a letter of sorts."

She handed Richard what could only be described as a scrap of paper and watched as his emotions flittered across his face.

Finally looking at Amelia, he grimaced. "I thought my father was the worst parent anyone could have, but it seems Mrs. Evans has taken the title from him. Read it; I can hardly believe such callousness."

Amelia took the scrap and read the tiny handwriting.

Girls,

These things will get you to London and hopefully pay your rent for a little while. I have decided that I have sacrificed enough, and I am pursuing my own happiness. I cannot be encumbered any longer with unmarried daughters.

You will need to find positions to earn your keep. Choose wisely, you are both pretty and could easily find yourself a provider willing to spend on you. Save all you can, for looks do not last forever.

Mother

Amelia sank onto the bed. "How could she write that?"

"It is not easy to read when you know the girls in question."

"She is telling two innocents to sell themselves. My goodness, I hope they never see her again! What a monster!"

Richard smiled slightly at her outburst. "We seem to be falling back into the habit of agreeing with each other as we did before."

"It is not a bad thing," Amelia said ruefully, for the moment at least relaxing because of Richard's calm manner. "What shall we do?"

"About us agreeing? Stop immediately."

"Brute."

Sitting next to her, Richard lifted her hand and held it in his; it was the most contact they had shared since kissing, and he smiled a little when Amelia looked at him in surprise. "I just need to reassure myself that there are decent people in the world who will stand by those who have been wronged. You were right to offer assurances to the girls, and I should have offered my support too. I too often think that everyone is selfish and out for their own advancement."

Amelia leaned into him, bumping his shoulder with hers. "There are many people like that; fortunately, we are not, but are left to clear up the mess of others. I feel heartily sorry for the girls, but apart from delivering them to their grandmother, there is little else we can do, is there?"

"We can find Claude and Mrs. Evans and force him to settle funds on them. If he has set himself up with the mother, he can be responsible for once in his life and look after the daughters."

"Do you think he will?"

"I can hope," Richard sighed.

"And we thought we were attending a simple house party."

"It is certainly not how I expected life would develop."

"No." There was nothing else Amelia could offer. She liked him far more than she had expected to, even when he was being cold and aloof, but she could not allow any closeness to develop.

Sighing, Richard stood. "I suppose the best we can hope is that we can be civil to each other."

"Can we not be friends?" Amelia asked.

Pausing before nodding, Richard turned to the door. "It will be easier to live under the same roof if we are. Goodnight, Amelia."

Closing her eyes briefly, Amelia knew that she was being unfair to him. She could not be a wife to him in the truest sense, so to expect anything from him was unreasonable, but she could not live with them barely speaking, or it would be a lonely life for them both.

Chapter Fourteen

THE VISIT TO the girls' grandmother went off more smoothly than any of them could have hoped. She took one look at the girls, and the three of them started to cry.

Amelia and Richard had exchanged a look, but the grandmother soon pulled herself together enough to speak.

"Thank you. Bringing them to me was the right thing to do," she sniffed.

"If you require anything further from us, please contact me. Here is my card," Richard said.

"You are very kind, but I will take responsibility for them from now on. If that mother of yours comes knocking on this door, she will be sent away with a flea in her ear," she said to the girls.

"I am hoping to find my cousin and persuade him to settle an amount on them," Richard said.

"There is no need; they both have a dowry. My husband left them an amount which will see them well settled when the time comes."

"We knew nothing about it," Laura said to her grandmother.

"If your mother had known there was a dowry settled on you, there would be nothing left; she would have found a way to access it. She could never live within her means, though I have been supporting her since your father died."

"You have not," Sarah said.

"I have, you little minx. Where do you think her money came

from? She ruined your father financially, but I was determined she was not going to take away what was rightfully yours."

"She told us you did not want anything to do with us," Laura said, clearly shocked once more by the actions of her mother.

"I did not want anything to do with her, but you have always been welcome. I do not think she wanted you to find out that I was not the ogre she portrayed me as. She was what back home we would call a tawpie, and she has never changed."

"She sounds very like my cousin. I think they are made for each other," Richard said.

"Until the money runs out," Amelia chipped in.

"You are right, Lady Douglas, but she will not find a welcome here."

"I never want to see Mama again," Sarah said.

"No need to get upset over something that is not going to happen. Thank you both for your escort. I am sorry you were troubled," she said to Amelia and Richard.

"Do not worry, we were coming to town to visit with my parents," Amelia said. "We will leave you be."

They were escorted out of the house by the group of three, constantly being thanked for what they had done. There was no mention of the stolen items. They had been given to Richard for return to their rightful owners, apart from the money, which Richard had said belonged to the girls.

As the carriage set off, Amelia sighed. "I can only hope that the visit with my parents will go as well as that one."

"Do I need to aim my quizzing glass in their direction?" Richard asked.

Laughing before becoming serious once more, Amelia shook her head. "No. Not at all. They will be disappointed that they knew nothing about you beforehand. I need to tell them that it was love at first sight and we were swept along by our emotions, or they will start to question me, and I would rather not tell them the real story."

"No. The fewer people who know about that the better, but will they believe your story?"

Amelia looked out the window, watching London life pass them by as they trundled through the busy streets. "I have always said that I would only marry for the deepest love." She said nothing else, and Richard did not respond to her words.

They continued in silence, and only when the carriage stopped did Amelia look at Richard again and take a breath. "I hope you are a good actor."

RICHARD HAD NO need to act; he was in love with Amelia. He was also angry, frustrated, and completely baffled by her. Knowing she was attracted to him was no comfort, for she was certainly keeping him at a distance, yet she had asked if they could be friends. The look of happiness she had sent in his direction when he had nodded his agreement had given him hope, but her words in the carriage had once more disheartened him.

Being welcomed into the house by a footman, there were suddenly squeals and shouts from above, and two girls thundered down the stairs.

"Amelia! You promised we could be bridesmaids at your wedding!" they chanted.

Embracing them both, Amelia smiled ruefully. "I just could not wait. I am sorry."

"We need to hear everything about it," the elder of the two demanded.

"I think I should introduce you to my husband first," Amelia said. "Richard, these are my sisters, Caroline and Lucy."

Bows and curtsies were exchanged, at which point they were

joined by Amelia's parents and further introductions were carried out.

"Come, we are being foolish standing around; let us go to the drawing room and you can tell us all about your adventure," Mr. Beckett said.

"If I could have a private word with you, sir," Richard said.

"Of course, but let us hear all the details about your meeting and the wedding first," Mr. Beckett said.

They settled into the drawing room, which was clearly that of a gentleman's abode rather than a wealthy member of the *ton*. The whole house was about half the size of Richard's, but was furnished well and with taste. Tea was handed out to the constant chatter of the younger sisters.

Richard watched the family interact with fascination. Neither Caroline nor Lucy resembled Amelia; she had rich auburn hair and storm-gray eyes, whereas they were blonde and hazel-eyed. Their features differed, and it increased his curiosity about the parents. They were a family who clearly thought highly of each other, all being very tactile, constantly touching each other in some way.

Even when Amelia started telling her story, her mother had sat next to her and was regularly stroking her arm or squeezing her hand. The fondness between them all was lovely to see, but also a little overwhelming to someone who had no experience of anything resembling the setting before him.

Richard could understand why Amelia had been upset that her parents would have found out about her betrothal through the newspaper. He cursed his cousin further, for causing hurt to the close family. Without doubt they would have been devastated to have been notified in such a cold way.

A longing to belong to something so warm built inside him as he listened to the fanciful tale Amelia spun to satisfy the curiosity and romantic notions of her family. There was never any condemnation from any of them about the way the marriage had taken place, though they clearly would have loved to have been there.

"Are you to live in London?" Mrs. Beckett asked.

"We have not decided yet. The Season is virtually over, so I suppose not." Amelia smiled. "With all the excitement over the wedding and then accompanying the Misses Evans to their grandmother, there has been little talk of what we are to do once we returned to London."

Richard nodded in support of her words. "Once the final entertainments are over, it would be nice to visit the family home."

"Oh, Amelia! We will hardly see you once you go to the country!" Caroline exclaimed.

"Of course you will, and just think, it is Lucy's turn for a Season next year."

"We are going to bring you both out together," Mrs. Beckett said to her younger daughters.

There were whoops of joy at her words, and Richard looked at Mr. Beckett. "Is now a good time to have that talk?"

"I think it is, for no doubt they will start to speak of gowns and all that nonsense," Mr. Beckett said, standing and leading the way to his study.

Richard followed him, and when seated opposite Mr. Beckett, he came straight to the point. "As we have decided that we will not be having children, my wife and I would be delighted and obliged if you would allow us to settle an amount on your younger daughters for their dowries."

Mr. Beckett did not answer straight away, steepling his fingers in front of him. Seeming to ponder Richard's words, he eventually sat forward, elbows on the desk. "That is a very generous offer and a surprising one, since I know Amelia would love a house full of children. Tell me, what is the real story behind your marriage to my daughter? And I would be grateful if you gave me the truth rather than the Banbury story my daughter tried to convince us with."

"Ah. I did not think you would be fooled."

"I was not. I think you had better start at the beginning." Mr. Beckett sat back, fingers steepled once more.

Richard knew there was no advantage in being anything but honest with his father-in-law, though he was still reeling to find out the woman who had rejected any physical contact with him wanted children. Was he really so repulsive that she could not face having children with him? The way she had sighed into him when being kissed did nothing but confuse him, and his head ached with constantly trying to work out what the devil was happening.

Being honest with Mr. Beckett became easier as Richard spoke. There was no condemnation in the older man's expression; he just nodded occasionally without interrupting.

"Amelia did not wish to upset you more than you would have already suffered, hence the tall tale," Richard finished. "Having seen how close you all are, I can completely understand her sentiments and am even sorrier that we are in this situation."

"It is not what I hoped for my daughter, but from your words, I can hope you will look after her."

"I will, sir, of that you have my word," Richard said solemnly.

"Thank you. My concern is that she will be unhappy. You say that you will not have children, but surely in time…?"

Richard could feel the heat crawl up his neck. "It is not my decision; it is something my wife decided on, and although I admit that I am not happy about it, I am not the type to force anyone into a situation they do not wish."

"Though it is your right as a husband," Mr. Beckett pointed out.

"I have enough examples of how to be a brute of a man from my father that I can assure you I detest any type of mistreatment of another. I might not like it, but I respect her decision."

Mr. Beckett nodded. "In that case, I am happy to welcome you to the family."

"Thank you, that means a lot. Now, if we can discuss finances."

When Richard returned to the drawing room, he smiled at Amelia's concerned look. "Your father would like a word."

"Is there anything amiss?" Amelia whispered as she passed him to leave the room.

"He demanded the truth, so I have told him."

Amelia closed her eyes briefly but set her shoulders. "I thought he might." Leaving the room, she entered her father's study. "What is this about you making demands of my husband already? Are you trying to frighten him off?"

Mr. Beckett stood and approached her. "If I know the truth, I can try to help."

"I do not need your help, Papa," Amelia said. "Everything will be well."

"Without your own children in your life?" Mr. Beckett asked gently.

"I am six and twenty; the chance for children is probably gone already," Amelia said. She tried to make her voice light, but she knew her father was not convinced by her tone.

"Do not stay with him out of obligation from being caught in an embrace. If you wish it, we could seek a divorce."

"No!" Amelia said hotly. "We could not afford the scandal or cost, and I could not put Richard through that. Yes, we are strangers, but he could have walked away after what happened. It was my fault that we were in that room, and he gave me the chance of not being kissed, so I am more to blame for this situation than he is, but he stayed and behaved like the gentleman he is. I will not repay him by causing him further upset."

"At least you both want the best for each other; that is as good a start as some marriages have. I hope you will be happy; it is all I have ever wanted."

"I know, and I thank you for it, but truly, we will find our way to muddle along," Amelia said, kissing her father. "You have not to worry about me."

"I will do that until my dying day."

When Amelia returned to the drawing room, there was no sign of Richard. "What have you done with my husband?" she asked her mother.

"Jacob arrived home and enticed him to have a game of billiards," Mrs. Beckett answered.

"It was more of a demand," Caroline said.

"Oh lord, I think I need to save him. He is as far from Jacob in character as he could be," Amelia groaned.

"Let the girls go." Mrs. Beckett nodded to her daughters, at which they eagerly left the room.

"I now feel really sorry for him." Amelia grinned at her mother.

"It is a good opportunity for us to speak."

"Oh dear."

"There is nothing to worry about. I wanted to say how happy I am that you have overcome your worries about being intimate with a husband. I told you there was nothing to concern yourself over if you met the right man."

Blushing beet red, Amelia choked out, "Mama!"

"We are both married women, which means we have a deeper understanding of the world and what marriage involves. I am sorry I was unable to advise you before your wedding night, but I hope that there were no problems. From the way his lordship looks at you, I am reassured."

"Oh, Mama," Amelia groaned, hiding her face in her hands. "There is no point hiding it from you because I know Papa tells you everything. We have not had a wedding night, nor will we be having one. I cannot let him see me."

"My dear child! I had hoped that would not be the case. Oh, Amelia!"

"It is fine, well, it isn't, but we have agreed. There is nothing more to discuss about the situation. I have now had two conversations with my parents that I never thought to have."

Shaking her head at her daughter, Mrs. Beckett sighed. "There is no point us starting an argument because I know full well how stubborn you can be, but please, if you hold him in affection, try to overcome your fears. I would hate to see you destroyed by him having liaisons with other women."

Amelia immediately thought of the woman who had rejected him, and she gritted her teeth. The thought of him... No, she still could not change the way she felt about intimacy. She would have to learn to turn a blind eye, even if it would slowly kill her if he did.

Chapter Fifteen

RICHARD CONDUCTED THE tour around his townhouse later that evening. They had left the Beckett family, promising to visit again soon, though Amelia was sure her cheeks were still stained with blushes at the conversations that had gone on.

"You have similar taste to your aunt," Amelia said as the tour ended and they returned to the drawing room.

Richard smiled briefly. "She told me to employ the same designer she had used, and though I do stand up to her sometimes, getting rid of signs of the past was what this house needed. It reminded me of my father more than the estate did."

"You really did not get along with your father?" Amelia was curious about his background; they had shared so little, but there had been hints along the way.

"No. I detested him," Richard admitted, frown immediately in place. "He was the most unfeeling brute you could possibly meet. He certainly believed that beating a child was the way to show him the right way."

Amelia winced. "That is awful."

"Yes, after my mother died, he got worse. I never saw him being kind to anything or anyone."

"You poor thing. It must have been a very lonely childhood."

"Thankfully, my aunt stepped in and rescued me. It probably saved our lives because I could see myself reaching breaking point if I had remained living with him. I would have killed him and then swung for it."

"I am glad you did not," Amelia said.

Richard looked at her thoughtfully before speaking. "You are very lucky to have a loving family around you. It was encouraging to see the open affection between you all, but I was surprised how different you look from your sisters and mother."

"Ah, yes, we cannot hide the differences, they are too marked. Jacob and I do take after my father, but Clarice is not our mother, though we do consider her as such. My mother died three years after I was born. I only have vague sensations of her rather than solid memories."

"I am sorry about that. I am thankful I can remember my mother," Richard said gently.

"Do not feel pity, please, for I have been very lucky; we all have. Papa mourned for a few years, but we had servants and a nanny who all cared for us in the best possible way. I can honestly say that I never felt anything but loved. When I was six, Papa brought Clarice home and told us that she was our new mama. I thought it was wonderful, but Jacob did not at first. Clarice had the patience to deal with the clingy child, which I was, and the child who was feeling threatened by her. She has since admitted it was the hardest six months of her life. I love her for herself, but especially for her patience with us. Jacob worships her, as we all do, and she has given us two lovely sisters and has made Papa very happy."

"I would never have guessed that she was not your mother, except for the difference in looks."

"Yes, the stories of wicked stepmothers are not always true." Amelia smiled. "She has never treated me as anything but her real daughter, and I look upon her as my mother in every sense."

"I am glad my father did not remarry; he would have just crushed another woman as he did my mother."

Amelia moved and sat next to Richard on the sofa. "I cannot imagine what you went through as a child, but I am sorry that you suffered."

"I always thought I was not a good enough son, and I confess thoughts like those have haunted me." Richard had never told anyone except his aunt the way he felt, not even Bea, so he was surprised to be uttering the words.

"Oh, that is such a sad burden for a child to carry! You poor thing."

Smiling at her, Richard said, "I survived."

"A child needs to do more than survive; it needs to be nurtured and loved."

"Most children are ignored by their parents; at best, they are brought down to guests to perform when they are nearing the end of their school days. I do not suppose I was too different from others in some respects."

Amelia placed her hand on Richard's. "I think you are making light of what happened, and I understand why you are doing that, but there was nothing you could have done to change the personality of a cruel man."

"Thank you," Richard said, turning his hand so he held hers and squeezing it. "Your words mean a lot."

They stayed in that position, staring at each other, almost as if they were nervous about ending the moment of closeness.

Bringing her hand up to his lips, Richard kissed it. "I would kiss you, but I do not wish to cause a breach between us."

"If it is just a kiss..." Amelia said.

Richard needed no further encouragement, pulling her onto his knee and kissing her with the passion that had built since their first kisses. Exploring her this second time was even better than the first. This time, he knew what would make her moan and lean into him, or what to do to make her pull at his hair.

Allowing his hands to travel across her body, she arched into him, and he had to stop himself from throwing her on the sofa, but he managed to keep one part of his brain sensible, though it was a struggle.

A knock at the door made them break apart, and Amelia stumbled to her feet, at which Richard muttered an oath before helping her while instructing the butler to enter.

"I am sorry to disturb you, but Mr. and Mrs. Grandison are asking to see you, sir."

Another oath was uttered by Richard before he stood up and strode to the fireplace. "Show them in," he growled.

Amelia was straightening her skirts, but looked at Richard in surprise. "You are inviting them in at this time of night?"

"It is Bea. I knew she would be our first visitor," Richard said with a shrug.

Amelia studied Richard for any sign of emotion at his words, but his expression was closed off. Remaining standing, she felt at a loss as to how to react to the lost love of her husband.

Bea walked into the room, her husband following dutifully behind her. "Richard, my darling! You went and did it! Congratulations! This is the woman who has replaced me, is it? How lovely to meet you."

"Bea, Edwin, please let me introduce the new Lady Douglas to you," Richard said.

Bea moved towards Amelia and looked her up and down. Amelia met Bea's gaze, watching with some amusement as she was assessed. Bea was a beautiful woman, but there were lines around her mouth and frown lines on her forehead; her eyes were a clear blue, but though her mouth was smiling, her eyes certainly weren't.

"My lady, what a pleasure it is to meet you," Bea said insincerely before turning to Richard. "I have missed you, my darling." She flung open her arms and embraced Richard.

Amelia saw him close his eyes briefly, and it was like a dagger being driven into her heart. Being told he was still in love with someone was completely different than seeing it in person. They had been kissing passionately only a few moments before, and now he was enjoying the embrace of another woman.

"Don't worry about those two," Mr. Grandison said. "They are like this all the time; can't keep away from each other. Bea insisted we visit the moment we saw the lights on. She's been driving past every day since you departed, my lord."

"I was convinced you would return early from your aunt's party." Bea pouted as Richard moved out of her embrace. "I admit I did not expect you to be wed."

"You are," Richard replied stiffly.

"But Grandison is so understanding." Bea smiled at her husband, who looked indulgently at her.

Richard turned away from Bea, gripping the mantelpiece. The room was silent for an uncomfortable amount of time before Bea moved once more to touch Richard.

"Oh come now, don't go all missish on me. You know you have a special place in my heart, and Grandison does not object to that. Do you, sir?" She was rubbing Richard's arm while smiling at her husband.

"I would never come between such good friends," Mr. Grandison chuckled.

Amelia could not believe that he was allowing such fawning towards another man by his wife. The warning that her mother had given her was ringing in her ears as she watched Richard accept whatever Bea decided to do to him. The party had remained standing, and Amelia refused to sit, though her legs were beginning to ache. She would not encourage this strange pair to stay.

Bea moved to her husband and kissed him on the lips. "You are the best of husbands."

"I do my best, my dear."

"And you do it so well. I hope your wife will be as understanding and indulgent as my husband is. I would hate for our *friendship* to alter." Giving a mocking look at Amelia, she crossed back to Richard and rubbed her hand across his back as he remained standing, turned partially away from them all.

Richard muttered something Amelia did not hear, but Bea laughed and moved away. "Grandison, Richard is being a grump tonight. You know how he is when he is tired. Let us leave him in peace, but we will invite the newlyweds to our house. It was a good thing I saw the notice of your marriage before we returned to the country; we were all ready to pack, weren't we, Grandison? I had accepted that you were not returning early, but I said we must stay because I want to see Richard as much as he will want to see me."

"You did," Mr. Grandison said.

"Goodbye, Lady Douglas. I am sure we will get on fine; it seems you will fit into our little group just perfectly," Bea said, an insincere smile on her lips. "We will send an invitation around tomorrow."

They left the room; the last thing heard was Bea's tinkle of laughter before the outer door was closed.

Richard remained at the fireplace, posture stiff, fist clenched, and Amelia soon discerned that he was not going to speak. She wanted to scream and shout at him but could not embarrass herself in such a way. Instead, she moved to the door, but before leaving, turned to him.

"I would expect you to conduct your liaisons away from our home. I have not been fair with regards to intimacy between us, and I can promise you that there is a very good reason for that, but please respect me enough not to flaunt anyone, and *her* especially, here."

"Amelia, I..."

"I do not wish to hear it, my lord," Amelia said, reverting to his formal title when they had been using their given names. "I would not believe whatever you said after that little performance. Goodnight."

Leaving the room and starting up the stairs, she heard Richard shout, "Devil take it," but continued on her way with a heavy heart and longing for the support and comfort of her family.

Chapter Sixteen

AMELIA HAD ASKED for a tray of breakfast in her chamber instead of facing Richard the following morning. She was not usually so cowardly, but having hardly slept and looking pale, she could not face a conversation with him before having some sustenance.

Hearing a commotion downstairs after she had finished enjoying honey cake, bread, and scones, she went to her chamber door, dreading that Bea had returned already.

"I need to see him! He's the only one who can help. Richard! Where are you?" Claude's voice rang through the house.

Hurrying downstairs, she followed Claude as he went into the breakfast room. Richard had said he usually breakfasted there informally when he was showing her around.

Claude turned when she entered the room behind him and looked surprised and then slightly amused to see her, but his smile soon fell, and he turned back to Richard.

"Bow Street are after me," he said, approaching his cousin. "You have to help!"

Richard had stood at his cousin's entrance, but his attention had moved to Amelia the moment she had appeared. When Claude gripped his arms, he was forced to stop trying to work out if Amelia was still upset from the disaster of the previous evening.

"Claude, what the devil are you doing? You have a blasted nerve coming here after the trick you pulled on myself and Amelia and stole from your mother," Richard said coldly.

"Never mind that! I am going to hang!"

"Your mother reported you to the authorities, has she? Good, you deserve all that you get. You have been nothing but a selfish thief. In fact, you are worse than a footpad; at least they do not know who they are stealing from. You stole from your own mother," Richard snarled at his cousin.

"It has nothing to do with Mother!" Claude snapped. "I was giving her a taste of her own medicine, that is all. Do you think me a total fool that I would steal everything and give away my heritage and my future?"

"With you, Claude, nothing would surprise me."

Flopping into the nearest chair, Claude put his head in his hands. "You have to help me, Richard. She is dead, and they are trying to blame me."

"Who is dead?" Richard demanded.

"Jessie," Claude moaned.

"Who is Jessie?" Richard asked in confusion.

"Jessie Evans, the woman I love," Claude answered before bursting into tears.

Amelia and Richard looked at one another in astonishment, all antagonism between them forgotten for the moment. Richard moved to the decanter on the side table, filled a glass, and gave it to his cousin.

"Drink this and tell us what on earth is going on."

Claude did as he was bid with regard to the brandy, but it took him longer to get himself under control enough that he could speak. Eventually, he looked at them. "I know what I am and what you think of me, but I do not want to hang for something I have had nothing to do with."

"For God's sake, Claude, you have come here for my help. I cannot do anything unless you tell me everything that has led to this."

"We came to London just to have a good time, and then I had

every intention of marrying Jessie and returning home. Mother would have been so grateful to get the deeds to the land back that I thought she would accept who I had chosen as my wife," Claude started.

Amelia and Richard shared another look. Neither thought that his mother would have accepted a marriage to Mrs. Evans, no matter what sweetener Claude tried to pacify her with.

"Did you marry her?" Amelia asked.

"No, it was supposed to happen yesterday," Claude said, once more looking close to tears. "She insisted on staying in a different hotel to me on the night before the wedding, said it would be bad luck if we saw each other, and she wanted everything to be right and tight between us."

"You weren't in your lodgings?" Richard asked.

"No. Mother would have been able to trace me if she had sent anyone after me. I thought you would be on the warpath, so I booked us into a hotel."

"I was going to find you, but it got delayed," Richard said.

"Exactly my point. She booked into a hotel a little off the beaten track, and I left her there two days ago, alive and well." Emptying the glass of brandy, he held it out for a refill, and Amelia took it off him, knowing that Richard would want Claude to continue with his story.

"What happened next?" Richard asked.

"I turned up at the church, and like a fool, I waited and waited. I could not believe that she would have deserted me at the altar; she was no Bea. I know what you felt like now, and I am sorry for ridiculing you for acting the mooncalf around her ever since. I would have done exactly the same with Jessie."

"Get to the point," Richard said through gritted teeth while Amelia handed Claude a refilled glass with unsteady hands.

"I went straight to the hotel and demanded that they let me into her room. They had seen me the day before and opened the door, and that is when we saw her." Claude choked again, but taking a large gulp of liquid, he tried to continue. "It was clear she had been attacked, had not died naturally. I will never forget the sight of her and all that blood."

"How does that relate to you being accused of her murder?" Richard probed, not unkindly.

"The blasted manager started saying that I was the only other one to have been in the room. Jessie had taken all her meals in there, so no one had seen her from when she arrived. He started shouting to get the magistrate, and I panicked and ran."

"That was not your finest idea."

"You try seeing the woman you love dead before you and then be accused of her murder and remain calm!" Claude snapped at Richard. "I have walked the streets since leaving that hotel, terrified of what was going to happen. When I talked myself into returning to my lodgings, there was someone watching the building, and that was when I knew that the only person who could help me was you."

"I would have no idea where to start," Richard confessed. "Other than to speak to the Bow Street Runners or the magistrate and try to get them to look at alternatives."

"That would be no use! They have already made up their minds. I cannot hang for this; I truly loved her and would never have harmed a hair on her head."

Amelia thought it time to step in. "Do you know of any reason that someone would want to hurt Mrs. Evans?"

"My mother?" Claude said dryly before becoming serious once more. "She said her husband's family disowned her when he died, but apart from that, no."

"We have met her husband's mother, and although we cannot be sure, I would be very surprised if she instigated something like murder," Amelia said. "You look exhausted, Mr. Greenwood. I think a bath and bed is in order, and we can have a think about what to do for the best."

"You have every right to throw me out and let me fend for myself, I am aware of that," Claude said to Amelia. "If it is any help, this has made me acknowledge that I have been the worst kind of son, cousin, friend, and protector, but I do not deserve to die for something I didn't do."

"We are where we are," Amelia said, ringing the bell and then giving instructions to the butler, who nodded and led Claude to one of the guest chambers.

"I would not have blamed you if you had thrown him out," Richard said.

"It would achieve nothing apart from causing a scandal, and no one wants that. I am not sure what to do other than to offer him a bed for now. Surely, Bow Street will soon check here for his whereabouts?"

"I would imagine it is only a matter of time. From the wording of the note to her daughters, I think Mrs. Evans was not as angelic as Claude would wish to think. Those were the words of a hard and worldly woman," Richard said.

"Yes, and one thing Bow Street will not easily find is the address where her daughters are staying. Mrs. Evans clearly presumed from her note that they would return to whatever lodgings they had."

"We are going to have to tell the girls their mother is dead," Richard groaned. "Damn Claude. I beg pardon; I seem to do nothing but curse in front of you."

"If you cannot be open with your wife, then it is a sorry state of affairs." Amelia's tone was sharp.

"I could respond in kind that the sentiment you have mentioned works both ways, but I do not wish to get into another argument. Should I go to break the news alone?" Richard asked. His tone was terse, but there was a hint of sadness in his eyes that Amelia could not fathom, but he was right; it was not the time.

"I will come with you. We will need to ask some difficult questions," Amelia replied.

"One day, life might be simple, but whenever my cousin is involved, it never is." Richard sighed, ringing the bell for the carriage to be brought around when they would be ready. "You are going to appreciate your family more and more as time passes, and I will be constantly offering excuses for mine."

BREAKING THE NEWS to Laura and Sarah was probably the hardest thing either of them had ever done. It was pitiful the way the girls crumpled into each other, distraught that their mother was dead. It was some time before they could gather themselves enough to speak coherently.

"I held no affection for Jessie, but I would have never wished any harm on her," Mrs. Evans said. "I am sorry to ask, but is there any chance your cousin could have been the one to murder her?"

"I have thought over it myself," Richard started. "I do not have a great deal of affection for my cousin, and I am the first to admit that he has many faults, but in this case, I believe he is telling the truth. He is devastated, had arranged the marriage, and was standing at the altar. I doubt even Claude could keep up such a farce, and there is no reason for him to act in that way. If he wanted to, he could just have walked away from any contact with Mrs. Evans; she had no money or anything that Claude would want. There is no motive on his part, even if they had argued. I have seen his reaction when that happens. He flounces off to sulk somewhere; he is not a violent man."

"You are right, there is no motive," Mrs. Evans said. "But who would have one? Do you think it could have just been an unfortunate instance of the wrong place at the wrong time?"

"The manager said she had not come out of her room, so she did not interact with anyone apart from the staff," Amelia said. "It all seems very odd."

"What is going to happen to us?" Sarah asked.

"You will remain with me until you find yourselves husbands. There has to be a period of mourning, but I am determined to see you well settled," Mrs. Evans replied.

"We were hoping that you might be able to tell us a little of your life in London, who visited you, where you stayed," Richard said gently.

Laura and Sarah exchanged glances before Laura started to speak. "Mama pretended a lot of the time. We lived in a very rough part of town, but whenever asked, she would always mention a nicer area. There was a sitting room and two bedchambers and a shared kitchen, but Mama managed to get invitations to many balls and gatherings, and she used to tell us to eat as much as we could at them."

"She used to slip some items into her reticule if she could," Sarah said.

"Would that include items of value?"

"I don't honestly know, but after stealing from your aunt, I would not be surprised. She never told us of anything she had taken, but we noticed that sometimes her reticule was a little fuller when we left," Laura said. "We were always terrified that someone would notice and cause a fuss."

"She was receiving an allowance from me, which would have enabled you to lodge in a nicer area," Mrs. Evans growled out. "What did she spend the money on?"

"From the sounds of it, creating a façade," Richard said.

"We visited the finest modistes, but she would never allow them to bring anything to us, we always had to collect everything, and she hired the finest horses for us to ride in Hyde Park," Sarah said.

"It was like living two lives." Laura sniffed, tears filling her eyes once more. "I hated living in the lodgings, especially when Mama told me not to speak to anyone or I would end my days ruined and living in the gutter."

Amelia looked at the older Mrs. Evans with some sympathy; the woman looked fit to burst. Whether it was anger or upset, she had no idea, just knew that she was as shocked as Amelia to hear the girls speak about the reality of their lives.

"It was exhausting," Laura said. "To get an invitation for a house party was almost heaven-sent. We could relax in some ways, though Mother kept on at us to secure a husband at whatever cost. She had even spoken about contriving a compromising situation, but then she started to be friendly with Mr. Greenwood."

"A perfect solution for her, security for the remainder of her days," Richard said.

"I am sorry for the insensitive nature of this question, but did your mother ever have male visitors at your lodgings or go and meet them?" Amelia asked. "It is just that in the note she left you, she did not seem too concerned with your being set up by a benefactor." She was not sure that her words were delicate enough to hide the horror of the reality of a mother willing to see her daughters as mistresses, but it was something that had to be asked.

"That woman!" Mrs. Evans muttered darkly. Laura flushed and looked embarrassed.

"We are not condemning her for anything; we are just trying to get a picture to see if there was someone who might have fallen out with her," Richard said gently.

"Tell them, Laura. She cannot curse us now," Sarah said to her sister.

"I do not remember everything, but recently, a few years ago or so, there was a man she thought was going to marry her, but they fell out when he revealed he had no intention. I don't think he was rich, though he did live in a better area than we did."

"That would not have been hard," Sarah said.

"We did not have a bad life, Sarah!" Laura said defensively.

"Whenever we stepped outside, we were in danger. If you did not feel it, I certainly did. No one else dressed as fine as us; they thought we had more than we did because of our clothes. I was always terrified until we climbed into a carriage and could leave everyone behind."

"It was a miracle you were not attacked!" Mrs. Evans said.

"I expected it every day," Laura said, giving Sarah a sad smile. "I tried to hide my fear, for I wanted to give you some courage if you saw that I was not afraid. Believe me, inside I was constantly scared."

"You poor children." Mrs. Evans hugged one after the other.

"Were there any more gentlemen?" Richard asked.

"There was one, but he never visited us; she met him somewhere in town."

"Did you ever know who he was?"

"No," Laura said. "She used to say Grand by name, grand by nature, but that was all. She did show us what he bought her, though: clothes, shawls and trinkets, plus the money."

"How long had it been going on?" Richard persisted.

"Two years? Maybe more? I do not really know. She did not expect this one to marry her, though. She said he was good enough for now, and they were both happy with the situation. She said he helped get her some invitations, a word here and there asking a hostess if his distant family could attend their event, but we were never introduced to him," Laura said. "Do you think he could have something to do with her death?"

"I have no idea," Richard answered honestly. "I am just trying to get a picture of your mother's life and who could have a motive to kill her."

Sarah burst into tears at his words. "I can't believe I will never see her again! It is too horrible! I know I said I did not want to see her, but I didn't mean it!"

"We shall leave you alone," Amelia said to Mrs. Evans. "If there is anything we can help with, please let us know."

"Thank you, but we will be fine together," Mrs. Evans said. "I just hope you can find out who did this."

"So do we," Amelia said.

Chapter Seventeen

ON THE JOURNEY back to Douglas House, Amelia could not help asking a question that had bothered her since Claude had uttered the words.

"At the risk of sounding insensitive and selfish with what is going on at the moment, can I ask you something personal?"

"You can."

"Did she leave you at the altar, as Claude said?"

Richard looked wary, but shook his head. "Claude is one for the dramatics. No, she did not, but it was close enough for me to look the complete fool. Everything had been arranged."

"That must have been hard."

"I was devastated, then angry, and then it was just another confirmation of not being good enough." Richard shrugged.

Staring at him in astonishment, Amelia could not help her words. "I cannot believe that you thought that! I would more likely find fault with the woman who had a man clearly in love with her and, after accepting him, letting him down."

"You are of a similar mind to my aunt." Richard smiled a little.

"In this, she is right. How long was it before she married Mr. Grandison?"

"About a month."

"There must have been talk."

"There was. I am surprised you did not hear it; it was in every gossip paper published."

"Ah, my injury again. Mama and Papa did not wish to upset me by reading about what was going on during the Seasons I missed, so there was a distinct lack of information coming into the house."

"They really did everything they could to help you, didn't they?"

"That is what families do."

"Good ones."

"Yes."

They lapsed into silence, but it was a more comfortable one as the carriage took them home. Amelia was saddened that she could not stir a great love in him because, even though he did not have feelings for her, she was desperately in love with him. The way things were, she did not know how to make anything better, and she was not sure about her ability to live with a man who loved another, but she accepted she had to try.

Arriving home, they had only just entered the house to be told that Mrs. Grandison was awaiting them in the drawing room.

"Bea's here?" Richard asked, closing his eyes for a second as if wishing himself away.

"She is allowed free rein in the house?" Amelia asked.

"Not really, perhaps a little," came the shamefaced answer.

"It gets better and better," Amelia muttered, striding to the drawing room. "Good morning, Mrs. Grandison. This is an unexpected surprise."

"Oh, please, call me Bea," Bea said, standing. She had a tea tray next to her, which also held an array of cakes. "After all, we are going to be firm friends. The tea is still hot. Would you like some?"

Amelia looked at Richard with raised eyebrows, a clear indication of what she thought of such a situation. To be offered tea in the home of which she was mistress was a huge insult for Bea to give, but Amelia just shook her head and answered through gritted teeth. "No, thank you."

"I know you will, my darling," Bea said to Richard. "I know what you are like if you do not have your required amount of tea in a morning. He can turn into quite the beast, you know." Bea stood and handed the cup to Richard, but then rested her hand on his arm.

"To what do we owe the pleasure of your visit?" Amelia asked. She could almost feel her hackles rising as Bea continued to stroke Richard's arm, and he just stood there stiffly and allowed it.

"Have you not told her about us, my dear?" Bea turned to Richard, pouting. "I thought I was your number one. We visit every day and compare where we are to go in the evenings. We like to dance with each other, and although my dear Richard can get a little silly sometimes, we do not like to be apart."

"Oh, you do, do you? I am surprised you never mentioned that, particularly as you know of my enjoyment of dancing," Amelia said, sending a message to Richard that the words had stung because of her inability to dance properly. She knew he had understood when she saw him flinch.

"Bea, sit down," Richard said.

"Only if you sit next to me," Bea said.

When it looked as if Richard was going to comply, Amelia could not stand it any longer. "Can I ask, Mrs. Grandison, why you wish to spend so much time with my husband when your rejection of him and marriage to another would suggest that he was not the man for you?" Bea glared at Amelia, of which she was glad. She would rather have a discussion without the pretend flowery words; they made her skin crawl. "I would also like to know why my husband, who you clearly hurt, puts up with this nonsense from you, which can only be described as leading him on."

"Amelia..." Richard said.

"I want answers. Now."

"She does not understand," Bea said to Richard. "You silly boy, you never told her. We love each other and always will, but I needed someone like my Grandison to give me exactly what I wanted in a husband, and Richard could not do that."

Amelia felt nauseous at Bea's words but refused to let it show. "And what was that?"

"My freedom. Being Lady Douglas, I could not have gone about town as I wished. I would have had to produce an heir, and that would not suit. This way, I can enjoy my time with Richard without the binds of rank, and my dear Grandison does not mind one little bit."

"Then he is a fool," Amelia said with derision. "Tell me, what do the wives think of you lying with their husbands? Do they turn a blind eye the way your dear Grandison does?"

"Amelia!" Richard choked out. "Your words are not appropriate."

"Are they not?" Amelia demanded. "You surprise me. I would think that a man who lies with a married woman does not really have a say on what is appropriate and what isn't. If you are happy to be the plaything of this woman and be ridiculed for it, that is your business, but you will not drag me into your degenerate ways!"

"How dare you!" Bea spluttered.

Amelia stepped forward until she was very close to Bea's face. "I dare because that is my husband, not yours, and this is my house, not yours. I will not tolerate you coming in and acting as if you own the place. From today, you will not gain entry into this house without my consent. There will be no waiting for us to return, no making yourself at home, for it is not and never will be yours. Now get out." Amelia had never been as angry in her life, and it was fired by the fact that Richard had not said a word to support her or stop Bea's outrageous actions.

"Richard! This is preposterous! Tell her!" Bea appealed to Richard.

"I think you had better go home, Bea," Richard bit out, and Amelia could only assume that his fury was because she had insulted the love of his life.

Bea looked between the two, and finally admitting defeat, she shrugged. "I will take my leave of you both, but I hope you can sort out this nonsense, for there is no need to change the way things have been."

As the door closed behind Bea, Amelia spoke through tightly gritted teeth. *"Go home, Bea?* That is all you have to say?" she demanded.

His face was pale and set. "I thought it best that you were not further tormented."

"You think I will calm down when I have just come to the conclusion that your mistress has the run of your house, and you expect me to behave like some sort of sap and accept her? You are such a surprise. In your aunt's house, you lorded it around, looking at everyone you disliked with derision and scorn, and yet with her? With her, you are nothing more than a bird-witted gudgeon!"

"It is not like that," Richard said heatedly.

"It is to me, and though it might be selfish, I refuse to accept this. A cold marriage was bad enough, but I accepted my part in that, but this? I cannot be usurped in the place I am supposed to feel most comfortable with the man I care about. I could tolerate some things, but sharing you with her? No. I am done."

"What do you mean?" Richard looked panicked.

"Exactly what I said. I am done. Excuse me."

There was no need to knock on Amelia's chamber door; it was open, revealing the sight of her pulling clothes from drawers and throwing them into a portmanteau.

"You are leaving," Richard said, feeling as if his world was spinning out of control.

"What else can I do?" Amelia demanded, only stopping long enough to glare at him. "I refuse to be made a fool of no matter what sort of marriage we have. Do you think I can stand by whilst you lay with another woman?"

"I may be being a numbskull, but as you wish to be my wife in name only, I do not understand why that would upset you so much."

Flinging the clothes she held onto the pile already in the portmanteau, she paused. "Just because I cannot have a true marriage in the real sense of the word, it does not mean I do not want to."

Stepping through the door, closing and locking it, Richard approached her. "Bea, nor anyone else, is a threat to you," he said gently.

"But she said..."

"I am sorry that I let you down so badly. I should have shut her up, but I was reeling from what she was saying. She has always dangled the promise of something happening between us, and like the fool I am, I hung around for scraps of her attention, but she had never been as open or suggestive of a real possibility of a liaison between us until now," Richard said.

Amelia turned away from him. "I understand if you still love her that it would be too much of a temptation, but I am sorry, I cannot stand by and know what is happening between you."

Richard gently touched her chin until she was facing him. "I could never do that to you. The reason I was so stunned was that I had expected such a proposition would have me running to Bea, smitten and with my heart open for her to crush, but the thought repulsed me. All I could think of was that you were being unforgivably insulted in your own home, and yet you defended me. You made a claim on me as your husband, and it made my heart soar." He smiled at her, moving a lock of hair behind her ear. "You see, I might have loved Bea once, but then I became locked into a situation I thought I wanted. I hated seeing Bea today, sitting in the drawing room and acting as if she owned the place. If I'd had my wits about me, I would have thrown her out."

"Would you really? This is not your attempt at pacifying me to save face, is it? To persuade me to stay, and then you continue a liaison with her?" Amelia wanted to believe him. She should have pushed him away and carried on with her packing, never to look back to this nightmare, but she cared for him, she loved him, and his words soothed her.

"There is nothing and never will be anything between Bea and myself; she missed her chance when she married Grandison. But more important than that, I do not want you to leave," Richard answered. "Everyone I love leaves. If you go, I do not think I could go on because I have never felt so in need of being with someone as I do with you."

The sincerity in his voice touched her, and her resentment seemed to burn away. "But I have let you down as a wife."

Richard pulled her to sit on the chaise lounge next to him. "What is really going on with that, Amelia? Your father told me that you had always wanted a houseful of children and he was shocked to hear that we were not to have any. Coming from such a warm, caring family, I can completely understand why you would be so inclined, and I do understand that we are strangers in some respects, but that is not it, is it? There is something else."

Dropping her head to look at his hands entwined in hers, she knew she had to be honest. It was time to be strong, as she always tried to be, but knowing what his reaction would be made the tears fall.

"I cannot bear for you to see me without clothes. I am monstrous," she choked out before dissolving into sobs.

Chapter Eighteen

"I DO NOT understand." Richard was truly flummoxed by Amelia's reaction. She got angry, she did not get upset, and it shook him almost as much as the thought of her leaving did. He could have killed Bea for last night and today; she was acting like some jealous schoolroom miss when she had no right to, and it had been weakness and confusion on his part that had prevented him from speaking out. He cursed himself for his inaction.

"Sarah was correct in what she said, I am maimed, and I cannot face the revulsion, from you especially, if you saw my true self," Amelia sobbed.

"What do you mean, me especially?" Richard asked, stroking her back, needing to comfort her, but at a loss as to what to do to stop her hurting.

"You are the one person I cannot abide the thought of viewing me with scorn, pity, or disgust. I would rather never lay with you and have a lonely marriage than face that."

"You think I would act so cruelly?"

"It would be perfectly understandable if you did."

"We are talking about your scars? From the injury?"

"Yes."

Richard took a handkerchief from his pocket and removed Amelia's hands from her face. "Is that what has caused the distance between us?" he asked, dabbing the tears gently from her cheeks.

"Of course it has!"

"Then I am justified in saying you are the numbskull, not I, if you thought I could be so unfeeling. It is also a little insulting," Richard said, genuinely upset that she would think so little of him.

"You have a reputation for the derisive set-down, which was relayed to me on more than one occasion," Amelia defended.

"I thought you knew me better."

"I clearly don't if you deny ever having slept with that woman, for I was convinced you had."

"I have not and never will. I can easily give you my solemn promise in that regard," Richard said seriously. "But I do not want to think of her again, nor let her come between us. I have longed for you since almost the moment we met; actually, no, it was the moment we met. I was supposed to give you a set-down for your comments about my quizzing glass, and instead, I stared at you like a besotted fool."

Amelia smiled. "You did not!"

"I damn well did," Richard said. Leaning in, he kissed her cheek to soften his words.

Sighing, Amelia looked down once more. "I do not want your pity as much as I dread your rejection."

Richard stood and pulled her to her feet. Putting his fingers under her chin, he lifted it until she was forced to look into his eyes. "I would never reject you nor pity you, my feisty, brave wife, but if you trust me enough, I want to show what it is to love you as you should be loved."

As she breathed in sharply, Amelia's heart rate increased. "But what if—"

"No. None of that," Richard interrupted. "None of us is perfect. Will you help me when I have nightmares and wake up crying, or will you ridicule me?"

"Of course I would not ridicule you! That would be cruel."

"True, but I never considered that you would, for I trust you to help and support me. Trust me in the same way."

"It is my own fears stopping me, and I am afraid to let them go."

"I promise I will not let you down."

"But I am scared," Amelia said, though she wanted him so badly. Her body was reacting to him, even though her mind was still fearful.

"So am I, because I never want to let you down, and I am flawed. Let me show you what pleasure awaits, but I promise to stop if you wish it."

"That is not fair on you."

"Being close to you is all that I need," Richard said, finally claiming her kiss.

The relief that flooded through him when she leaned into him made him pull her against him. She felt comfortable, as if she was meant to be there, yet there was immediate passion between them. He trailed a finger down her spine, and she shivered at his touch, wrapping her arms around his neck and gripping his hair.

As he moved to explore her jawline and neck, he whispered, "I might never cut my hair. I love the way you make demands with your hands in it." Amelia chuckled, but heat crept up her cheeks. "I need you, Amelia. I want to make everything perfect between us."

"It is."

"Oh, my love, this is nothing," he murmured, moving to her lips once more. Starting to slowly unhook her dress, he felt her stiffen slightly. "If you want me to stop, you say, and I will," he breathed onto her lips. Her eyes were wide, pupils dilated as she looked at him. Breathing heavily, she nodded and was rewarded with a warm smile. "We are going to take this very slowly, and you will not regret it."

Carefully undoing each button while still kissing her, he loved how she melted into him. He wanted her so much he ached, but he would make sure there were no regrets on her part.

A banging on the door and rattling on the door handle made them jump apart before remembering that the door was locked.

"Go away!" Richard commanded.

"Richard! Bow Street are here! I need you!" Claude shouted through the door.

Leaning his forehead on Amelia's, Richard sighed. "My blasted cousin. I think I will let Bow Street take him. At least then he will not spoil anything else."

Amelia laughed, her breathing not yet into its normal rhythm. "We have to help him."

"Five minutes, Claude!" he shouted. "I suppose we do, but once this is over, I am banning him from this house for at least six months."

"Will you be sick of me by then?" Amelia teased.

Roughly kissing her before turning her around so he could refasten the buttons he had undone, he continued to kiss her neck as he worked. "If I lived to be a hundred, I would never have enough of you."

"Is it not too soon to be making such grand statements?" Amelia asked, self-doubt creeping in once normality was resuming.

"I could have easily said something similar by the end of the first meal when we were seated together," Richard said, turning her back to face him. "When my leg brushed against yours as I sat, it was like my body had come alive for the first time, and when you touched my arm, I felt you claim me. If that sounds fanciful, then I can only assure you it is true."

"You were affected too?" Amelia asked.

"Oh yes. Now let us go and sort my cousin out, and then we can continue." With one more quick kiss, Richard put her hand on his arm, and they walked to the door.

"LET ME GET this straight," Richard said to the Bow Street officer as they all sat in his study. "You are here to arrest my cousin for murdering his wife-to-be because the manager of the hotel says he was the only one seen with Mrs. Evans?"

"Mr. Greenwood was the only person to visit her," the officer replied.

"That you know of. I hardly think that someone who wanted to commit murder would announce themselves, do you?"

"Well, no, but who else would want to harm Mrs. Evans?" the officer replied, not being cowed by Richard at all.

"Why would her future husband, the one waiting at the church for his bride, with the clergyman no less, want to have harmed her?"

Claude had been sitting quietly, looking pale and afraid, but at Richard's words, he jumped up. "I loved her! She was the only one in the world who cared for me. Why in damnation would I want to hurt her?"

"Perhaps that quick temper of yours made you lose control, and being at the church was a clever ploy?" the officer said with a smug expression.

"I doubt any of us would be calm if we had just lost the woman we loved and were now being accused of her murder." Richard intervened before Claude could cause any further issues for himself.

"Have you checked if anything is missing? Could it have been a robbery?"

"If Mr. Greenwood could give me a list of what Mrs. Evans took with her to the hotel, I can check if her belongings are still in place."

"Claude, go to the breakfast room; there are writing materials in the desk at the window. Make the list and try to think of everything," Richard said.

"Why can't I make it here?" Claude asked, clearly not willing to leave the room.

"I want you to concentrate. If we continue to speak, it will only distract you." The officer seemed to want to object to Claude leaving the room. "My cousin will not do anything foolish; he only ran away out of shock," Richard said. "You have my word that Claude is not going to run again."

"I have nowhere to run to," Claude said, but left the room.

"You will have to excuse my cousin a little. He has never felt so much for anyone in his life, and to have her taken away so brutally, he is struggling." Richard glossed over the way Claude seemed unable to utter anything other than words to make him look guilty.

"Begging your pardon, my lord, but anyone who is guilty acts in the same way as Mr. Greenwood does; they commit the crime and then don't want to hang for it."

"I am sure they do not. There was another reason why I wanted him out of the room. I wish to speak candidly, and what I have to say can only upset Claude further, but might give you some information that will aid your investigation. For it is still an investigation, is it not? I would hate to think that you have already come to the conclusion that my cousin is the killer."

"He is the main suspect."

"I hate to speak ill of the dead, but when we told her daughters of Mrs. Evans's death, we also asked about her—relationships," Richard said.

"She has kin? The manager said he had never seen her with any family when she visited."

Amelia and Richard exchanged a look before Richard turned back to the officer. "Yes, she has two daughters who she abandoned at my aunt's house when she ran away with my cousin. She had stolen from a number of the guests who were staying with my aunt and had accused one of the maids of stealing, though it turned out she had hidden the missing item herself. I do not think Mrs. Evans was the paragon of virtue she tried to make out to be; she suggested her daughters find themselves a protector to look after them and put the stolen items in their luggage."

Remaining quiet, the officer was clearly mulling over Richard's words. Eventually, he looked at Richard, more resigned than he was previously; clearly the case was no longer as clear-cut as he had thought. "The manager said Mrs. Evans was a regular visitor to his establishment," he confirmed.

"Mr. Greenwood could not understand why she chose that particular hotel, for it was not in the best area, he said. He had asked her to stay somewhere nicer, but she had refused. She obviously had a reason to go there that Mr. Greenwood knew nothing about," Amelia said, speaking for the first time.

"But why the night before her marriage?" Richard mused.

"To say goodbye to someone? A protector of her own from what her daughters said," Amelia answered.

"They knew who was supporting her?" the officer asked eagerly.

"No," Richard replied. "Unfortunately, they never met the man, nor did their mother name him."

"Though she did say he gave her grand gifts. Grand by name, grand by nature, were the words repeated to us, so whoever he was, he was a generous benefactor," Amelia said.

"That could mean it's any of the toffs," the officer muttered. "They can all be generous until it is time to cast someone off."

Amelia saw Richard stiffen and had to hold back a smile even though it was a serious topic. "Can the manager give some indication of who the gentleman might be?"

"No. He said the staff are taught to be very discreet."

"When a man could hang for a murder he did not commit, I think discretion has to be forgotten," Richard said.

"Until you are the man who needs to be protected, then you would not feel the same," the officer responded tartly.

"Thankfully, that is not the issue here," Amelia said, trying to contain what could quickly turn into the Bow Street officer being thrown out if the thunderous expression on Richard's face was anything to go by. "I do think it would be useful if you could use your experience and tact to find out who was meeting Mrs. Evans before she became attached to Mr. Greenwood."

"I can assure your ladyship that I will leave no stone unturned," the officer said magnanimously.

"Then I know we are in good hands." Amelia smiled at him.

Claude came back into the room and handed a list to the officer before helping himself to a glass of brandy.

"Is that wise?" Richard cautioned.

"After that task, yes," Claude replied, sitting heavily into his seat. "It has just brought everything back."

"If I could ask a question, Mr. Greenwood?" the officer asked, list in his hand and frown firmly in place.

"Go on," came the resigned answer.

"You are sure Mrs. Evans had a sapphire necklace?"

"Yes. It was my wedding present to her. She said that she was to wear a rich blue dress, and I thought it would go perfectly. I had to admit that it was a little damaged on one of the patterns. There is a diamond missing, but she didn't mind."

"There was no necklace or any other item of value in her room," the officer said.

"What? Then she was robbed?" Claude asked. "Oh God! How she must have suffered!" He started to sob and, discarding the glass, held his head in his hands.

"I need to search Mr. Greenwood's things," the officer said to Richard.

Richard shrugged. "He came here with the clothes he stood up in, so you can search his person and his room by all means."

"Where is his luggage?"

"I am presuming still in the hotel he was staying in."

"Is that right, Mr. Greenwood?"

"What?" Claude sniffed.

"Your luggage is still at your hotel?"

"Yes, but you are not searching it without Richard being there." Turning to his cousin, he appealed with red-rimmed, watery eyes. "There is too much important documentation and jewels for someone not to be there, but I cannot go back."

"You left it in the room? For anyone to find?" Richard asked incredulously.

"I did not think I was going to be away from it for so long!" Claude defended himself. "Only for Mother's sake do you need to be there. I could not care less if I never saw any of it again."

The officer was clearly interested in the exchange, but did not make comment about it. "My lord, I would like to carry out the search as soon as possible."

"Then we shall go immediately." Richard stood and rang for the carriage. "Claude, please remain with Amelia."

"I am not going anywhere, so you can all stop worrying." Claude snapped at his cousin. "I haven't done anything wrong."

"You ran once, sir," the officer pointed out unhelpfully.

"That is because I panicked. Would you like to see what I did? My future wife, dead!"

"I did, sir, and I grant you that it was not pleasant."

Claude looked green. "Just go and sort this bloody mess out. Get the person who did this and make them swing high and long for what they did to my Jessie."

Chapter Nineteen

DURING THE AFTERNOON while waiting for Richard's return, Amelia filled her time with writing letters and answering invitations. A lot had been sent to them since the announcement in the newspaper, and she was hard-pressed to decide on what entertainments they should accept.

She worked on the desk in what was her private study. The room was slightly smaller than Richard's own study, but was more to her taste, furnished with comfort in mind but practical, with an outlook over the garden. While she was engrossed in her letters, the butler interrupted her.

"My lady, I have a note, which the delivery boy says requires an immediate reply," the butler said, lowering the tray so that Amelia could take the card.

Reading it, she sighed. "Will that woman never take a hint?" she muttered to herself, then looked shamefacedly at the butler. "Sorry. I should be more ladylike, shouldn't I?"

With twitching lips, the butler bowed his head slightly. "Sometimes, my lady, it is good to be open about one's frustrations, and you can be assured of my discretion in all matters."

"Thank you." Amelia smiled at him. "If only you could advise me on what to do for the best in this situation. I have no idea how long his lordship will be."

Coughing slightly once more, the butler bent his head towards her.

"If I could offer…"

His words trailed off, but Amelia responded quickly. "Any advice will be gratefully received. You know the characters involved, I do not."

"If you are attending events at Mrs. Grandison's home, she cannot be making you uncomfortable in your own home," the butler said.

"You are quite right. I just wish I could avoid her completely."

"I think once Mrs. Grandison accepts she no longer holds any power over his lordship, she will lose interest in pursuing any friendship with either of you. I hope I do not speak out of turn, my lady."

"You do not," Amelia said. "And you are quite right. I just hope she loses interest soon."

"She is testing at the moment."

"Yes, she is," Amelia sighed, but smiled when the butler choked in an effort to hide his laugh. "Thank you for your advice. I will accept the invitation." Scribbling a note, she leaned back in her chair once the door was closed and she was alone again. "You are not going to win this, Mrs. Grandison. You had your chance and you squandered it."

Hearing Richard's voice, she quickly got up and went to the hallway. He was alone and handing his hat and cane to a footman.

"Is Claude nearby?" he asked, crossing the hall and kissing Amelia.

Blushing at his action, she shook her head. "He went to his chamber when you left. I think he is grieving quite severely."

"In that case, come with me. We can leave Claude's troubles for now." Taking hold of her hand, Richard started up the stairs.

"But it is late afternoon, and we are due at the Farringtons' ball tonight," Amelia said, allowing herself to be led.

"Oh blast! Am I ever going to get you alone?" Richard stopped at the top of the stairs. "I am happy to show off my beautiful wife, but I would much rather stay at home with her."

"Is now the time to admit we are to visit the Grandisons tomorrow evening?" Amelia asked.

Richard groaned. "Are we? Again, I would rather not."

His words warmed her heart, and Amelia smiled at him. "A wise man said she will soon tire of seeing us."

"I hope so. I suppose at least she isn't coming here, for my wife is fierce." Pulling her into his arms, he kissed her. "And I would not have her any other way."

Amelia let the doubts about what was inevitable drift away as she was kissed with passion and yet gentleness. She seemed to be in a permanent state of wanting to touch Richard and be touched by him. For someone who had forced herself to accept a lonely life, it was a heady mix to now think she might have a happy marriage.

RICHARD HAD DANCED with Amelia twice at the Farringtons' ball; he had not danced with anyone else. They had chosen the two least energetic dances, but it had still caused her pain. He could see from her pale complexion that she was hurting, and he wanted them to return home, but she would not hear of it.

"You can dance with others," Amelia said. "I do not mind. Well, I do, but that is my unreasonableness, not yours."

Richard laughed. "It pleases me to know that, but I assure you there is only one person I want to dance with in this room, and I have already done so."

"How could I ever have guessed that you could say the sweetest words?" Amelia teased.

"It is you bringing out the best of me." Squeezing her hand, he looked up to see Bea and Edwin bearing down on them. "Brace yourself, Amelia. Our peace is about to be disturbed," he whispered before turning to smile at the pair.

Amelia almost laughed at Richard's words and knew her eyes

betrayed her merriment as she greeted the people she wished far away from them both.

"Richard, my darling! I thought you weren't attending tonight or I would have claimed my dance earlier," Bea said, moving to give him a kiss on the cheek, but he side-stepped her and reached over to shake Edwin's hand.

"Do not fret, Bea. I am not dancing anymore this evening," Richard said. "Grandison, you are looking well."

"How could I not be with my wife by my side?" Edwin responded genially. "But I would like to take the opportunity to dance with your wife. It will let you two catch up. I know how you like to gossip."

"I am afraid I will have to decline your kind offer," Amelia said. "I am unable to dance for the rest of the evening."

"Are you unwell?" Bea demanded, looking between Richard and Amelia with some alarm.

"No, I am fine, but I have an old injury which prevents my dancing quite as much as I would like."

"Oh." The look of relief on Bea's face would have been comical, but Amelia was in no frame of mind to find amusement in the fact that Bea was relieved that Amelia was not increasing.

"Then let me take you for some refreshments," Mr. Grandison said, offering his arm to Amelia. "I have a proposition I would like to discuss with you that would be to both our advantages."

"We had just decided to leave. I cannot think of any offer you could make my wife that would necessitate us delaying our departure." Richard's voice was firm, clearly not happy with whatever was being suggested. He moved his arm around Amelia's waist. "I am afraid I wish to keep my wife all to myself tonight. We will bid you goodnight."

Bea shot daggers at Amelia, but without another word, Richard guided Amelia through the crowd and out into the hallway once they had said goodnight to the hostess. While they waited for their carriage to arrive, Richard stood, arm still around Amelia while she rested her head on his shoulder. There was no regret about leaving Bea; his motivation had been to prevent Grandison from taking Amelia from him. Was it jealousy? Perhaps a little, but it was also protectiveness. He knew Amelia would be suffering from the two dances, and he needed to make sure there were no long-lasting effects, for he wanted to dance with her again.

When they were seated in their carriage, and Richard had pulled a blanket over their knees, Amelia finally spoke. "You have upset Bea."

"Who's Bea?" Richard asked, wrapping his arm around her shoulders and tucking her to him.

Amelia laughed. "You are wicked. It was clear she wanted to speak to you alone."

"Then she is to be disappointed, for there is nothing she can say to me that cannot be said in front of you. I should never have indulged either of our foolish actions for as long as I did. I owe Grandison an apology."

"It is strange that he does not seem to mind the way she is with you."

"She has already admitted that she could not be with me because I would have demanded her be faithful, more fool him if he is willing to put up with that." Richard shrugged. "But enough of them, I would rather talk about the two of us."

"Oh?" Amelia immediately flushed.

"Yes, today has been a long day, but I would like it not to be over quite yet," Richard said, slowly pulling one of the clips from her hair so he could twist it through his fingers.

"Nor would I," Amelia whispered, blushing furiously at her forwardness, but she wanted to be kissed by him, held by him, though a part of her still feared his reaction.

"Good." Richard took his time kissing her. There was no hurry, they were in the carriage, and he was not going to do anything inappropriate for the servants to see. It was a pleasure to feel unrushed and explore her once more. Teasing her, nibbling her lips, and making her sigh, had his pulse racing with need, but he held back.

When the carriage pulled to a stop, Amelia looked dazed, and he smiled at the effect he had on her. Jumping out of the carriage, he reached in and held out his hand. "Come, my lady, we are home."

Amelia loved this Richard. There was no longer any sign of the aloofness she had first seen; he was constantly smiling and teasing her. It was as if the person he had been was someone else, and she hoped she was seeing the real man.

Walking into the house, still holding her hand, Richard looked at the butler. "I do not care if my cousin burns the house down; we are not to be disturbed. Am I clear?"

"Yes, my lord."

"Richard!" Amelia hissed at him as they walked upstairs. "I am never going to be able to face him again!"

Laughing, Richard squeezed her hand. "We are newly married. He would expect nothing less."

"I am mortified!" Amelia groaned.

"Soon you will not care who sees us or hears us come to that."

Choking on a laugh, Amelia covered her face with her free hand. "You are terrible."

"Only with you." When they reached Amelia's set of rooms, Richard stopped at the door. "I am going to go to my dressing room, and if you will allow me, I will join you in a few minutes."

"Yes." Amelia bit her lip, and Richard groaned at her action.

"Then again, we could just go straight in…"

"No! My maid will be waiting. I will let her take down my hair and then dismiss her."

"Wonderful idea. I love your hair down."

Amelia was reminded of the way he had looked at her in Mrs. Greenwood's house when her hair had been loose, and she felt even more breathless. This was it, she was going to give herself to this man, scars and all, and it was terrifyingly exciting.

Walking through the doorway, she looked over her shoulder at Richard one last time before closing the door. Their dressing rooms were joined through a sitting room, so Amelia knew he would enter her room that way.

Nodding to her maid, she immediately walked into her dressing room. "Just take my hair down and help me out of my dress, and that will be all for the night." Trying but failing to stop her cheeks from burning, she did not meet her maid's gaze through the looking glass. This was all new and more than a little daunting.

Chapter Twenty

RICHARD, DRESSED ONLY in his breeches and shirt, walked into Amelia's chamber and stopped. She stood, arms wrapped around her middle, chemise the only item of clothing she wore, hair tumbling around her shoulders and down over her back.

"You are beautiful," he whispered as he crossed to her.

"There are far prettier women than I," she said self-consciously.

"Not in my opinion," he said, reverently touching her hair. She closed her eyes as if afraid to enjoy his touch, and he gently moved her hands away from her middle. "I would much rather these were around me."

Smiling, she moved towards him, her hands running over his chest and around his neck. "Like this?" she whispered.

"Exactly like that," he replied before kissing her. He took his time exploring her body over the material, although he longed to tear it off and cast it aside. Instead, he pulled his own shirt over his head and threw it away.

With widening eyes, Amelia took in the broad chest with just a smattering of dark hair. If she had been told he worked the land, she would have believed it, for he looked even larger and stronger than he did when dressed. Mouth going dry, she reached out to touch his chest. Smiling at his sigh, she continued to explore him, stepping forward and leaning so she rested her head on his shoulder. Gently kissing his body, she was delighted when he groaned with pleasure, wrapping his arms around her as if wanting her to be even closer.

She did not think that they would ever be close enough. Reaching up once more, she looked at his eyes, which were a rich blue, no hint of the ice they usually contained. "Kiss me," she whispered against his lips, and he complied willingly.

When he moved her so she stood against the bed, she stiffened a little, but as he teased her neck, her jaw, her lips with kisses, she knew she could never stop him. He had already lit something inside her, and no matter what the end result was, she had to see it through.

The moment he looked at her for permission as he tugged at her chemise, she nodded and watched with wonder as he tossed the garment away and gazed at her with a reverence she could barely believe. He stroked her body with infinite tenderness, uttering endearments all the time. Eventually, he sought her eyes once more, the last question he would ask.

"I want you," she said. She had no idea what was to happen next, but the feeling of need inside her was driving her on. She wanted to be released, though from what she could barely imagine. Pushing her gently down on the bed, he only paused to tug off his breeches before climbing next to her.

She had never thought she would give herself to anyone, but with Richard lying so close, teasing her and tempting her, she willingly surrendered to her feelings, forgetting the worry and sadness that had haunted her since her injury.

"I never want this moment to end," Richard said, his hand trailing sparks of awareness as it grazed along the length of her. "You are perfect."

"Please do not say things that are not true," she begged. She could not accept falsehoods from him.

He rested his head on hers. "I am not uttering false platitudes. I do not care if you are scarred from your head to your toes; you are beautiful to me. I want you more than I have ever wanted anyone else, and that is the truth, too, before you dismiss it."

Amelia wasn't convinced by his words, but as he started to kiss her once more and his hands explored further, not another thought formed. Instead, she could do nothing but focus on wherever he touched her, experiencing sensations that made her gasp with shock and pleasure. That her delight was Richard's too was in no doubt as the world tumbled and shattered around them.

Afterwards, she lay curled into Richard, his arm around her, pulling her as close as could be. It was late in the night, and the house seemed to still around them as their breathing eased into a more regular rhythm.

Richard lazily stroked her arm as he watched the embers of the fire grow smaller. He had never felt such contentment, and he was almost afraid to move in case it broke the spell. "Thank you," he finally said.

"What for?" Amelia asked. Her voice was husky with exhaustion, but she lifted her head and rested it on her hand on his chest so she could look at him.

"For making me feel like I belong somewhere. I have not felt this content for a long time," he replied.

The slow smile that crossed her face made his insides feel lighter than he thought possible. "You will always belong here with me," Amelia said.

"Good. I was speaking the truth when I said I did not want this to end."

"Can we stop occasionally to eat?" she teased.

Chuckling and squeezing her, he dropped a kiss on her head. "Anything for you, my lady."

"Would you stay here with me?" she asked, lifting her head up.

"I do not understand."

"Here. In this bed. Would you stay with me?"

"Every night?"

"Yes." Amelia had to ask the question; the thought of him leaving her to go to his own room was intolerable. "I know it is foolish, but I feel like I could take on the world with you next to me. I feel whole again."

"I am glad of that, and of course I am going to stay. Why would I go to my cold bed when your lovely warm body is in this one?" Richard said, a lazy smile on his lips. "Now go to sleep or you will be exhausted in the morning, and I want you fully awake."

"You want more?" Amelia asked.

"I will always want more," Richard nuzzled into her neck. "But for now, at least, you have nearly killed me, and I need to recover."

Playfully swatting him before snuggling back into him, Amelia was asleep within minutes. Richard waited until her breath had the steady rhythm of deep sleep before he kissed her head once more and allowed his own eyes to close, a smile on his lips.

∽

ONLY APPEARING DOWNSTAIRS just before morning visits were to take place, Amelia could not take the smile off her face. The morning had been as loving as the night had been, and only when she had forced Richard to get up did they finally part. It was a wonderful way to start the day, and she was only a little bit embarrassed to know that everyone who saw her would be in no doubt as to what had happened.

Richard had gone into his study feeling lighter than he could ever remember, and even when Claude sought him out and then the Bow Street officer arrived, his mood was not affected.

"I thought I'd give you both an update, your lordship," the officer said.

"That is appreciated. You can imagine we are keen to find out who did this," Richard replied.

"When I went back to the hotel and started to make suggestions that one of the staff might have been involved in robbing Mrs. Evans, the manager was a little more helpful with his information."

"Blast the man! He would have seen me hang for something his staff had done!" Claude growled out.

"Not so fast, Mr. Greenwood," the officer cautioned. "I was using the ploy to make him willing to share what he and the staff knew, and it worked."

"You know who her *friend* was?" Richard asked.

"Friend? What friend?" Claude demanded.

Before Richard could come up with something to pacify his cousin, the officer spoke. "It seems before Mrs. Evans met you, she used the hotel for meeting with a gentleman friend," he said. "I am trying to find out who he is."

Claude turned on Richard. "You have started a lie!"

"Of course not," Richard said calmly.

"You will do anything to destroy what memories I have of her, won't you?"

"Claude, the information came from her daughters. What possible benefit would I have in spreading lies when they would only be discovered as such by this officer?"

"It is true, Mr. Greenwood, the hotel staff has confirmed it. Mrs. Evans met a gentleman there every week for the last two years."

Claude sank in his chair. "Then I was one of a long list of fools."

Taking pity on his cousin, Richard stood and walked over to him, putting his hand on his shoulder. "She was going to marry you, Claude. Never forget that; the other one was probably just a means to an end. Don't condemn her, because she cannot tell you the truth of the matter." He did not mention that she had wanted to marry another man; there was no benefit to admitting that.

"I just want her here," Claude moaned.

"I know, but finding her killer will have to be the next best thing. That is all you can do for her now," Richard said before returning to his seat. "What information did you glean from the hotel?"

"Other than that, I am afraid very little. The gentleman was an older man, jolly and a good tipper by all accounts. He gave a false name, but always paid his bill with cash, never credit."

"He really did not wish to be traced," Richard said.

"No, but one of the maids did see him near the hotel the night Mrs. Evans was killed," the officer said. "She said he entered through the side door, but she didn't see him go to Mrs. Evans's room or leave."

"He must have! Why else would he have been there!" Claude almost shouted.

"She must have sent for him for some reason," Richard mused. He disliked the way Claude sagged at his words, but it was the only way the stranger would have known Mrs. Evans was there.

"You think she was going to desert me?"

"I actually think the opposite," Richard said. "She was marrying you; there was nothing in her actions to suggest she intended doing anything else, and that is supported by the note she left her daughters. I think it is more likely she was breaking off whatever arrangement she had with the gentleman."

"And he did not take kindly to that," the officer agreed.

"He would kill someone for that? And then rob her?" Claude asked incredulously. "There are women aplenty who would welcome such an arrangement; he could have found someone else."

"We do not know his state of mind; he could have been in love with her for all we know but tied to another. At this point, we can only speculate."

"The chances of finding him are slim to impossible," Claude said.

"Now, sir, begging your pardon, but I am not giving up so easily. If I can't find the gentleman, I am going to find the jewels. One way or another, we will track him down, but I would still ask that you remain close by," the officer said.

"I am still a suspect?" Claude looked thunderstruck at the suggestion.

"Of sorts. I need to get everything right and tight, and then you can go off with my blessing," the officer said.

"Well I'll be," Claude responded, shaking his head.

"Thank you for updating us. You are clearly a man who gets results," Richard said to the officer. "My cousin will be staying with us for the foreseeable future; you have nothing to worry about in that regard."

"Thank you, my lord. I will be in touch as soon as I have more to report."

The door had barely closed when Claude started to mutter, "I am still being accused of murdering the woman I love! I cannot believe the audacity of the man!"

"Stop being so dramatic. He is doing his job and is coming around to the idea that it was not you."

"And I should be grateful for that?"

"Actually, yes, you should. You are in danger of slipping back into old habits, Claude. I would advise you to start thinking about how you will deal with your mother."

"She will never forgive me and will make my life hell. I think there is nothing for it but to move abroad."

"I would find a role on stage if I were you, with such tendencies for over-exaggeration as you have." Richard shook his head at his cousin. "Your mother has been wrong in the way she has lorded over you; I think what you have done will prove that she needs to change, but so do you."

"You should be on a pulpit somewhere with the way you preach," Claude muttered, making Richard laugh.

"Perhaps I too have missed my calling, but you have a chance to make things better; I hope you do not waste it."

Chapter Twenty-One

As they lay in bed the following morning, Richard traced his fingers along Amelia's body. She was lying on her side facing him, slowly waking up from another night of lovemaking. While she was in such a relaxed, only half-awake state, he could look at her legs without embarrassing her.

White lines of scars criss-crossed both legs, some deeper than others, clearly where the horse had bitten hard. He barely stopped the shudder at the thought of how close she must have come to death after such an attack.

"They are disgusting, aren't they?" she whispered.

Looking at her, he saw the sadness and vulnerability as she met his eyes. "There is nothing disgusting about you," he whispered, running gentle fingers across the scars. "But I am sorry you were hurt so badly." He cupped her face and kissed her gently.

"It was my own doing. I cannot even blame the horse, as I had been warned to stay away from him. Now I have a daily reminder of my foolishness and how grotesque I am."

Scowling at her, Richard pushed her onto her back and loomed over her. "I never want to hear those words on your lips again, you are nothing of the sort, and I will not have you uttering such lies."

As she tried to turn away from him, Richard effortlessly lifted her around to face him. "Let me go! I hate it when I know you are just trying to pacify me."

"Why the devil would I do that?"

"Because you are trying to make the best out of a bad situation." Tears filled Amelia's eyes. "I am sorry, but I cannot be her, and I am never going to match up to her."

They had spent the evening with the Grandisons, and though Richard had used every trick he knew without giving her a direct snub, in an effort to keep her at arm's length, Bea had still been suggestive enough to have caused them both discomfort. Richard had been grateful that Amelia had made him promise to spend every night in her bed, or he was convinced she would have escaped him when they returned home. Fortunately, or so he had thought, he had managed to take both their minds off the evening in the most pleasurable way.

Richard felt he wanted to shake Amelia until she understood, but he also appreciated the feeling of not being good enough; he had suffered from that all his life. "I do not want her. In fact, I would be delighted if we were never to see them again. I never noticed before what an absolutely demanding, draining, self-centred person she was until we returned to town. Now that I have got the best woman alive, I can see that my aunt was right all along. I would have been miserable as hell with Bea."

"I am sorry," Amelia said, wiping her eyes. "I just hate myself so much, and she seems so perfect, and I want everything to be well between us."

"It is wonderful. And, to me, you are perfect. These last few days have been my happiest, apart from last night when we were forced to go out. I think we should remain in this chamber for at least the next year to give everyone the message that we only need and want each other."

Amelia smiled. "That is tempting."

"Good." Richard kissed her, and just when he knew she had put aside her worries and melted into him, there was a knock on the door. "Go away!"

The knock was repeated, and Amelia pulled away, making Richard groan in frustration and flop back on the bed. Covering herself up, Amelia pushed at Richard. "Find out who it is!"

"And then cast them off without a reference, most certainly," Richard said, swinging his legs off the bed and walking to the door without stopping to put any clothes on.

Amelia was horrified and amused in equal measure when it was the butler at the other side of the door. Looking abashed at disturbing his master, he muttered something, and with a nod, Richard closed the door and leaned against it.

"My blasted family!" he groaned, pushing himself up and returning to the bed. Crouching over Amelia, he grimaced. "I am sorry, but do not think this is finished. I want to get you back to bed as soon as I can."

"What has happened?" she asked as Richard planted a chaste kiss on her lips and started to walk to the door of her dressing room.

"My aunt is here."

"Oh lord! And I am still in bed!" Amelia groaned, pushing back the covers and ringing for her maid. "What will she think?"

"That I am a very lucky man!" Richard called as he headed to his own dressing room.

The words were enough to make Amelia smile and relax a little. It would be mortifying that Mrs. Greenwood would know exactly what they were doing, but Richard made her feel so good about herself that she was willing to put up with the other woman's scorn.

Walking downstairs, Amelia could never remember feeling happier. She loved Richard to the point that she thought she could burst. She wanted everyone to know, especially her family, but she could not reveal anything just yet. He had not declared his love for her, and she would not push him. She believed that he cared for her and that had to be enough for now. Hopefully, over time, he would come to love her.

"Good morning, Mrs. Greenwood," Amelia said, walking into the drawing room.

"More like good afternoon," Marie said with a raised eyebrow.

Amelia blushed, but nodded to the footman who had followed her in with a tea tray. "This is an unexpected surprise. Are Mrs. Leaver, Patricia, and Isabelle returned with you?"

"They accompanied me, but decided to leave you be for today. I wanted to speak to Richard, not anticipating that Claude was here. That was a surprise, and not a good one from my son's reaction," Marie said.

"You have seen Claude?"

"Oh yes, and he will not forget it in a hurry." Marie seemed to soften after she had uttered the words. "I am being unfair. I could see he was shocked to see me as I was to find him here, but I can see that he really cared for that woman, and I am sorry that she has been killed."

"Yes, it is a horrible situation," Amelia said, pouring the tea. "At least it seems that he is no longer being considered as a serious suspect."

"I would have roasted every officer in Bow Street if he had been arrested. I am surprised Richard did not send for me."

"I suppose he would have if he thought there was any real risk of an arrest."

"Hmm," Marie said, accepting the cup and taking a sip. "You seem to have settled in to your new life."

Amelia laughed. "I would not go that far, but I hope that I have not embarrassed my husband too much at the events we have attended."

"And has that woman been around?"

"Yes, until I demanded she leave the house," Amelia said straight-faced. The crack of laughter her words caused brought a smile to her own lips.

"I am so sorry I was not here to see that! I bet she was furious,"

Marie said, still chuckling.

"I do not think she was too happy, but we attended their party last night, and she was still in top form, though a little more reserved than she had been. I still wanted to scratch her eyes out, though."

Marie laughed gleefully. "Oh, you are perfect! The sooner she accepts that Richard is not fawning over her, the sooner she will leave you alone. She has to be top dog, that one."

"I cannot understand her husband," Amelia admitted. "It irks me, and I have only seen it a couple of times. How can he stand it?"

"He is a fool for doing so. Anyway, enough about them. How is Richard?"

"I am fine, thank you, Aunt," Richard said, walking into the room and immediately crossing to embrace Marie. When he had welcomed her, he returned to sit next to Amelia, planting a kiss on her lips before she had time to react. "What brings you to London? There is very little left of society here."

"I came to look for Claude. I did not expect to find him here, and no notice of that fact from you."

"It was not my place," Richard defended. "As I keep telling you, he is a grown man, and I have offered him a place here as it helped to pacify Bow Street if he stayed with us."

"I had a long chat with him before I got bored and demanded that you be told of my arrival. That butler of yours did not want to disturb you."

"We did not want to be disturbed," Richard replied.

"Richard!" Amelia hissed, blushing deep red and causing Richard to smile mischievously at her.

Marie waved her hand. "Do not worry, he is trying to shock me more than you, but you would have to do more than that, boy. I have been around too long."

Richard smiled at his aunt. "Of which I am glad. What have you done with Claude? Is he attacking my brandy already?"

"No, you insolent pup. He told me everything, and I suggested that he sit down with you and go through what you have been doing for our estate. It is time he took on the responsibility."

"What about your concerns over his spending?"

"I have had to accept that he was acting the fool, yes, but I was not helping. I have never given him any responsibility, and it is time I did. If he squanders it, then we will both have learned a hard lesson, but after what has happened with the Evans woman, I do not think he will."

"It is the right decision," Richard said.

"As you have been telling me that for years, you can gloat all you like," Marie said.

"Not at all. In fact, where is Claude now? There is no time like the present to start handing things over, and it might help to take his mind off what has happened."

"He said he was going to read over the papers that he took from my safe," Marie said.

"Perfect. If you will excuse me, ladies." Kissing Amelia again before leaving, Richard did not see the smile on Marie's face at his actions.

"You have done wonders for that boy," she said to Amelia. "I hoped to see him happy and relaxed, and I admit that I thought you were wrong for him, but it seems I was incorrect with that too."

Amelia cursed her cheeks for flaring up again. "I think we are doing each other some good."

"I am glad to see it; his father was a brute."

"He has only mentioned a little about it."

"I know he tries to forget it and hates to think he could turn out like his father but be assured, there is not a cold-hearted bully within him, or his father would not have had such a large impact on his life. He might have been my brother, but I wished him to the devil."

"I cannot believe that a parent could be cruel to their own child."

"And that will make you a good mother. I hope you are prepared to reassure Richard that he will be a good father, for he is terrified he will make the mistakes his own father did."

"That is a little daunting."

"You have never struck me as a wilting wallflower," Marie said with a raised eyebrow.

Laughing, Amelia put her cup down. "No, I have never considered myself as such. I am sure we will work through it together."

"That is the best way, just keep talking to each other."

They were interrupted by an apologetic butler. "My lady, I am sorry to disturb you, but Mr. and Mrs. Grandison have come to call."

"Will they ever take the hint?" Amelia groaned.

"Let us make sure they are in no doubt of being unwelcome after today." Marie grinned at Amelia.

"Show them in," Amelia said to the butler, bracing herself for what was to come.

Chapter Twenty-Two

BEA WALKED IN, carrying a large bouquet of flowers. "I brought these for you. I noticed that you have very few adornments, and I said to Grandison that I am in the best position to give advice on such matters, did I not, my dear?" she asked over her shoulder at her husband, who was following her dutifully into the room.

"Thank you," Amelia said, accepting the large arrangement before handing them to the butler. "Can you do something with these, please?" she asked. "And a fresh tea tray would be appreciated."

"Of course, my lady," the butler said, quickly leaving the room.

Marie was staring at Bea with the fiercest expression on her face. "Is there something amiss?" Amelia asked her. Marie had said that the Grandisons would be aware they were not welcome, but Amelia was surprised at the ferocity of the glare Marie was aiming at Bea.

"I will say there is!" Marie growled out. "Why is this woman wearing my sapphires?"

"I beg your pardon?" Bea said, her hand immediately on the jewels around her neck in a protective gesture.

"I want to know why you are wearing my necklace," Marie almost snarled.

"How dare you, you silly old woman! This was a present from my Grandison, wasn't it, my dear?" Bea glanced at her husband for reassurance.

"It was." Gone was the usual jovial man as he watched Marie

closely.

"You are mistaken," Bea snapped.

"My sapphires are a very specific design, one that I chose myself, and there is a diamond missing on my set, right there," Marie said, pointing to where there was a tiny gap in which a diamond should rest.

"Nonsense! My Grandison explained that it had come loose and it was going to be sent for repair, but I liked the design so much that I wanted to wear it today," Bea said, clearly offended.

"I do not care what you have been told, child; that necklace is mine," Marie said.

Amelia had been staring at the necklace, and she suddenly looked at Grandison, who was still near the door. "Grand by name, grand by nature," she said in dawning horror.

There was a moment of stillness, but then he turned to the door, slamming it shut and turning the key. "That is a real shame. I had hoped we could become as friendly as my wife is with your husband. It would have been the perfect solution, don't you think? But it seems my actions are catching up with me. A pity, for you are a spirited young thing. I would have enjoyed our time together."

"Grandison, what is going on?" Bea screeched at him.

"Oh, shut up, Bea! For once in your life, be quiet, and I might spare you."

"What the devil do you think you are going to do in the house of a member of the aristocracy?" Marie demanded.

"That depends on your nephew, I suppose," Grandison said. He brought a large, folded knife out of his pocket and walked over to Amelia, roughly dragging her to him as she edged away. "You are the most valuable to his lordship, something my foolish wife did not wish to acknowledge, for she is blinded by herself when anyone can see how much he is smitten with you." Grabbing Amelia by the arm, he put the knife to her throat. "Behave, and you might come out unscathed."

"Grandison! What are you doing? I do not understand why you are behaving like this," Bea appealed, no longer the over-the-top fluttery woman, but looking terrified at her husband's actions.

"It seems I have been found out." He glanced with annoyance at Marie. "How did Jessie get your necklace? Did she steal it?"

"My son gave it to her to wear on her wedding day," Marie answered, sounding as calm and collected as she always did.

"Jessie? Who is Jessie?" Bea asked.

"The woman your husband has been seeing every week for the last two years, and I am supposing he is the man who killed her," Amelia said, and felt the knife press harder into her neck. Wincing in pain, she felt a trickle and guessed that the knife had broken the skin. Perhaps annoying and taunting him was not her finest idea, but she was furious for the three women now at his mercy, for the worry Richard would go through as soon as he worked out what was going on, and for Jessie, who had not deserved to die.

"You have a mistress?" Bea cried out.

"Of course I have, you stupid doxy! Do you think I was going to meekly accept you flaunting yourself at any man who took your fancy? You should be grateful that I did not behave the way you did," Grandison snarled at Bea.

"But you are old!"

Amelia bit her lip to stop herself from laughing at the comment and the subsequent growl the words caused. She exchanged a look with Marie, but was distracted by a pounding on the door.

"Do not come in if you want your wife to live!" Grandison shouted.

The pounding on the door increased. Amelia hoped that they would not use a different key to open the door, for she had no idea what Grandison would do, and she could not bear the thought of Richard being in danger. "We are well," she shouted, hoping to calm whoever was on the other side of the door.

At her shout, the pounding ceased, but there seemed to be a lot of movement in the hallway, though it was not clear enough to determine what was happening. Worried that Richard would put himself at risk, she sent a look of appeal to Marie.

Seeming to grasp some of what Amelia was thinking, Marie spoke. "What do you want to achieve by all of this?"

"I want safe passage from the house and the guarantee that I will not be followed. I might have to take you with me to ensure that," he said, yanking on Amelia's arm.

"Richard will follow you to the ends of the earth if you take his wife," Marie said conversationally. "If I were you, I would stop this before it goes any further. I really cannot see you coming out of it unscathed."

"That is a risk I will have to take. Her ladyship knows what I did."

"You murdered Jessie," Amelia said quietly. "But I do not understand why." One thing she did know was if Grandison took her out of the room, she would not live a moment longer than she was of use to him.

"She was laughing at me," Grandison snarled. "Saying that she did not need any more assignations or invitations from me, for her husband-to-be loved her, and they were going to live happily in the country."

Amelia saw Marie close her eyes in pain and understood why. Jessie was no angel, but she clearly loved Claude. "You killed her because she had found happiness?"

"She showed me the necklace, saying that I had never given anything so fine. She had the gall to suggest that I should increase the value of gifts I gave my next mistress if I were to keep her."

Amelia sighed. "She was foolish and probably heady at the thought of securing a good match at her time of life; you still had no right hurting her."

"Don't you preach to me!" Grandison pressed the knife harder once more. "She deserved what she got. I had given her far more than I should, and this was the way she repaid me? Discarding me for a younger man!"

"She found a husband!" Marie said.

"She could have still kept up with me, but no, she did not want to."

"I did not give her enough credit," Marie said to Amelia.

"None of us did," Amelia replied.

"Isn't this just a cozy scene," Bea spat at them, getting off the sofa she had sunk onto. "My husband pining over a hussy who was going to walk away from him. You deserve to swing for it." She started to walk towards the door. "I have had enough of this. Do what you wish with her, but I am leaving—you and this room."

"I will kill her if you touch that door," Grandison warned.

"I really do not care," Bea said, her back to the group.

"Bea, if you ever want Richard to speak to you again, I would think carefully before you attempt to leave," Marie warned. "He is besotted with Amelia, and she makes him happy; you have seen that, just as the rest of us have. I have only spent an hour in their company, and I could see it. Do not be a fool. If you think anything of Richard, any morsel of affection left over for him, then do not put Amelia at risk."

Bea stopped, still facing away from the group, her shoulders heaving. Finally turning around to face them, she looked at Amelia. "I am doing this for him, not you."

"Why did you marry me when you clearly still love him?" Grandison snapped. Amelia tried not to swallow, for in his anger, the knife was once more pressing uncomfortably on her skin.

"Because I could still have my freedom with you. Richard would have stifled me." Bea shrugged.

"Do you care for me at all?"

"You will never know," Marie said, picking up a vase and swinging it at his head.

RICHARD AND CLAUDE were disturbed from their conversation in the library by a very worried butler. "My lord, we seem to have a problem," the butler said.

"What is it? Is her ladyship well?"

"I don't know, my lord. Mr. and Mrs. Grandison called, and her ladyship allowed them entry. Mrs. Grandison bought flowers, and her ladyship asked me to deal with them and supply a fresh tea tray. As I was walking away from the room, I heard Mrs. Greenwood say something about a necklace. I must admit I did not think anything of it, but soon afterwards, the door to the drawing room was slammed shut and locked."

"What the devil?" Richard said, standing.

"A necklace? My mother said something about a necklace?" Claude asked.

"Yes, she was speaking to Mrs. Grandison."

"Richard, I have a bad feeling about this," Claude said, crossing to the door.

"I have taken the precaution of sending a footman around to peer through the window," the butler said.

"Good," Richard said. "This is out of character, even for Bea."

The three men walked into the hallway but did not approach the door as the footman came in, pale faced and panicked.

"What is it?" Richard demanded.

"It's the gentleman, my lord. He seems to be holding onto her ladyship, almost as if he has some weapon," the footman said.

Richard flung himself at the door, pounding on the wood as if strength alone could break it down.

They heard the words that Grandison shouted, which only increased Richard's actions. When he heard Amelia's voice assuring them that they were well, Richard turned to the others. "We need a plan because I cannot wait outside this door whilst my wife is in danger in there."

"Send for the Bow Street officer," Claude said to the butler. "And get out some pistols."

"You are not going to wave a gun around when we do not know what weapon he has. Your mother is in there too," Richard pointed out.

"I know, and I intend for both of them to get out in one piece, and that blaggard is going to hang for what he did to Jessie."

"We do not know if he did it," Richard reasoned, sounding unconvinced at his own words.

"There was talk of my mother's necklace. There is only one necklace missing, and the person who took it must have murdered Jessie," Claude said. "I would love to shoot him myself, but I also want to see him hang."

Richard nodded. "If he hurts Amelia…"

Claude touched Richard's arm in support. "We will do all that we can so that she is unharmed."

"Thank you."

The butler returned with a pair of pistols and handed them to Claude. "They are loaded, sir."

"Good. I am going to go outside and position myself so that if I get a clear shot at him, I will disable him."

"I know you are a good shot, but through glass?" Richard asked.

"It is the only way I can get a shot at him. There would be too much confusion if we did manage to break the door down, and who knows what he would be able to do in that time."

Richard looked sickened. "Fine, but leave me with one of the pistols. If he comes out this way, he will have me to deal with."

Claude handed him a pistol and left the house. All the footmen in the house were gathered in the hallway, along with the butler.

"What do you want us to do, my lord?" the butler asked.

"I have no idea; just be ready to act. Have you a key?"

"Yes."

"Then be ready to unlock the door if I say so," Richard said.

They waited, giving Claude time to put himself in position, Richard feeling that the whole house would be able to hear his heart pounding. He had suffered neglect and abuse, but he had never felt as helpless as he did now. He could not bear the thought of Amelia being hurt any more than she had already, but it was more than that.

He had found someone who he was content, happy, and in love with. As selfish as it sounded, he could not stand the thought that she might be killed. Without Amelia, he could not go on, and he had never told her that he loved her. He was a fool for not being open with her, and now he could do nothing to help her.

Hearing a crash and a scream inside the room, he shouted to the butler to open the door as the sound of a gunshot and breaking glass reverberated.

Nearly bursting the door off its hinges as it opened, he ran into the room, gun at the ready.

Chapter Twenty-Three

RICHARD STRUGGLED TO see what was going on; all he wanted to do was seek Amelia out and get her to safety. Grandison was on the floor, writhing in agony; Marie was standing over him, a vase held over her head as if ready to strike. Amelia was on the floor, partly obscured by a chair, and he moved towards her.

Bea accosted him. She had been huddled on a sofa, but sprang up on seeing Richard. "He was going to kill us! Oh, Richard, I am so glad you came!" she wailed, flinging herself into Richard's arms.

Richard struggled to unhook her grip on him as he still carried the pistol. "Bea, for God's sake, release me!"

"But I am afraid and upset!" Bea wailed. "I need you! My husband is a murderer!"

"I need to get to my wife," Richard ground out.

Bea looked at him, her surprise at his rejection loosening her grip, which enabled Richard to side-step her and move to the back of the chair. "But…" she said, not finishing her sentence and sinking back onto the sofa.

Richard reached the chair as Claude entered through the door, having run back into the house once he had made his shot. Handing his unused pistol to his cousin, Richard nodded towards Grandison. "It seems you and Aunt Marie make a good team."

Claude grinned at his mother. "You hitting him with that vase made me want to laugh so much, it would have affected my aim. You were magnificent, Mother."

"There is life in this old dog yet," Marie said, smiling at her son. "Good shot, Claude. I saw you outside and guessed what you were aiming to do. It was perfect timing because my strike would not have kept him down for long."

Claude seemed to grow under his mother's praise and took the vase from her. "I think you can take a seat for now. I will make sure he hangs for what he's done, but it will not prevent me shooting him again if he tries anything. There are so many limbs to choose from, which I can aim at but not kill him."

Grandison whimpered at the words, but did not try to sit up. Blood oozed from a shoulder wound, and he kept his unhurt arm on the back of his head where Marie had struck him.

Richard had crouched down near Amelia, unable to speak on seeing the blood on her neck and dress. When she looked at him, those storm-gray eyes he loved so much wide and frightened, he finally found his voice. "She needs a doctor!" he shouted, crawling past Grandison's legs to reach her. "Amelia, Amelia," he cried. "Where are you hurt?"

The pain and fear in his voice made Amelia reach out to him. "I am well," she choked out.

"But the blood is soaked into your dress." Richard was at her side but almost afraid to touch her.

"I think he has nicked my neck, that is all," Amelia said.

Taking his handkerchief out of his pocket, he wiped the blood from her neck and nearly sagged with relief that, yes, there were cuts, but they were shallow and already drying up. "You still need a doctor," he said gruffly. "You have to be well."

A tear tumbled onto Amelia's cheek, though she tried to ignore it. "I thought I would not survive. He had nothing to lose," she whispered.

"Dear God, if I had lost you," Richard choked out and enfolded her into his arms, rocking her, though they both sat on the floor. "I have never been so frightened in my life at the thought I could not reach you. I do not think I will ever be able to let you out of my sight again."

Amelia chuckled at his words. "You will soon get sick of me if you do not."

Richard pulled away from her just enough to look her in the eyes. "If I live to be a hundred, I will never tire of you. Believe me when I say that you are more precious to me than anything else. This is probably the wrong time, and I do not expect you to feel the same, but I have to tell you that I love you, Amelia. I think I have from the moment I was introduced to you, and I will love you for the rest of my days."

"Why would you not think that I felt the same?"

"The way we were forced into marriage, the nonsense and misunderstanding around Bea."

"I understand that you loved her and probably always will," Amelia said.

"No, no, no," Richard muttered. "I did, yes, I would have married her, and we would have been unhappy. For me, it was infatuation more than anything, and then hurt and the desire to make her regret walking away from me. She is nothing to me now. With you, I know life is going to be interesting; a challenge, yes, but also passionate and long-lasting. I can live with that, hoping that one day you love me as much as I love you."

"Oh, Richard, you silly nodcock, of course I love you!" Amelia had clasped his cheeks in her hands. "I would have been the happiest woman alive to have married you if I felt worthy of you. These blasted legs, but it seems I have married a very silly man who does not care that I am not perfect, and I love you all the more for it."

Richard kissed her, unable to speak, and ignored his cousin's cough until Claude shook him. "What?" he growled to his cousin.

"As much as your words sound as if you are reading from a romance novel, there are other things to take care of. The Bow Street officer is here."

Richard turned towards his cousin and, with some surprise, noticed that Grandison was now sitting on a chair, his wound strapped up by the doctor who had arrived, the Bow Street officer standing over him. Marie had also moved, setting his highly expensive vase back in its place and drinking tea as if it was the most natural thing in the world to do after being at risk from a murderer.

Claude was looking in amusement at Richard. "I think it is time you moved. The doctor is waiting to attend to her ladyship," he said, nodding at Amelia.

Helping Amelia stand and wrapping a protective arm around her waist, Richard led her to a seat and remained by her side while the doctor checked her over; all the time she reassured Richard and the doctor that she was well.

When assured that there would be no long-lasting scarring, Richard turned to the Bow Street officer. "Get him out of my sight."

"Yes, my lord." He lifted Grandison by his injured arm, which made the man yell out in pain, and he was taken out of the house.

Once he was gone, Claude sank into the space Grandison had vacated and put his head in his hands. "I cannot believe she died because she was about to get married."

Marie crossed the room and sat next to her son, putting her arm around him. "She was foolish in the way she taunted him, but she did not deserve his reaction. I am sorry, boy, I misjudged both of you and should have never tried to interfere."

Claude looked up at his mother. "What am I going to do without her? I never met a woman who I cared for like I did Jessie."

"Do not think of that now. It has all been a shock. I think a trip abroad might be in order. Not to forget her," Marie said quickly when it looked like Claude would object. "Just to give yourself time to grieve without the gossip and constant reminders. I know what it is to lose someone you love, and believe me, being active is the way to make the pain bearable."

"Will you accompany me?" Claude asked.

"Would you want me to?" Marie was clearly surprised by her son's request.

"I think it would do us both good."

"Then I think we should not wait until that scoundrel hangs; just knowing he will is enough. Let us start to plan our journey." Marie stood and held out her hand for Claude's. When he put his in hers, she kissed his hand. "I am sorry, son."

"It is going to be well," Claude said, and putting her hand on his arm, he nodded to Richard and Amelia and left the room with his mother.

"I am glad they are going to overcome their differences; it will be the making of them both," Richard said.

"I think you are right," Amelia said, leaning into him. "Where is Bea?"

Richard looked around the room, half expecting to see Bea, but apart from the butler, the room was now clear of people. "I have no idea."

"My lord, I thought it wise to escort Mrs. Grandison to her carriage and instruct the coachman that she might wish to visit her parents for a while."

"Good idea, the gossip will torture her," Richard said.

"In danger of sounding wicked, I think she will revel in the notoriety," Amelia said.

"Did you hear that?" Richard said to the butler. "My wife has a cutting tongue. I am to have a terrible life. Oof." He laughed as Amelia dug her elbow into his ribs.

"I am going to change out of this gown. I think the best thing is for it to be burned. I will never wish to wear it again," Amelia said with a shudder.

Richard helped her to her feet, though she protested at his fussing. The butler left the room, and Richard smiled down at her. "I think I need to help you out of your dress."

"Oh really?" came the arched reply.

"Yes, I also think that we are not open to visitors for at least the next sennight."

"A sennight?" Amelia said weakly.

"At least," Richard said, kissing Amelia and pulling her against him.

"Richard, sorry to interrupt…" Claude's voice came from the doorway.

Richard stopped kissing Amelia, resting his head on her forehead and closing his eyes. "Claude, why do you always seem to sense when we want to be alone and disturb us nonetheless?"

"It is a talent, I suppose," Claude said with a shrug.

"We have one thing we want to say to you," Richard said, looking at his cousin.

"Oh?"

"GO AWAY!" they both shouted at him.

Laughing, Claude closed the door and walked away.

Epilogue

Four years later

AMELIA PULLED THE blanket closer as she looked at the view, tumbling hills as far as the eye could see, but it was the playful scene in front of her that took her attention.

Richard was running around the flattened area at the top of the hill, two children squealing, trying to catch him. Laughing as he fell to the ground, they threw themselves onto him, babbling about their success in capturing the monster.

Stroking her swelling stomach, she smiled at her family. "It will not be long before you join your brothers," she whispered. She was enchanted by her children, who were growing up confident and happy in a loving household with regular visits from friends and family.

The *ton* saw them as something of an oddity: parents who actually enjoyed their children and spent far too much time with them. It seemed strange to those beyond their circle, but came as no surprise to those who were closest to them.

Richard and Amelia did not care what anyone else thought. Amelia brought up her children with the same affectionate devotion she had received from her parents. And though she knew Richard sometimes had doubts about his abilities, his children would grow up knowing how much they were loved by their father. He supported them in every way, determined to make them feel the security and love that had been absent from his life.

Only when Richard begged for mercy did the boys run into the folly and start to chatter to their mother.

"You are my brave soldiers." Amelia smoothed their tousled heads, one dark mop and one auburn. "I expect you are hungry now." She indicated that the nursemaid should take them to be fed in the only other room on the ground floor.

Richard came inside and flopped on the sofa next to his wife. "Am I safe?" he asked, kissing her.

"For now. You are not as attractive as food, but they will soon recover," Amelia answered.

"In that case, I had better make the most of my reprieve." Richard kissed her once more. "Are you comfortable?"

She smiled at him. "Of course. I have done this before, you know."

"Until he or she is born and I see you are well, I never rest easy," Richard admitted seriously.

"I know." Amelia wished there was some guarantee she could give him, but she was over thirty, and they were both aware of the risks of childbirth. This child might be their last, whether a boy or a girl. Although Richard had hinted that a sweet girl to complete their family would be a blessing. Amelia's self-esteem thrived under her husband's adoration, and Richard's bad memories had faded as they were replaced by new, happy ones. Created, he insisted, by the woman who always inspired him to be the best man he could.

"I think we need to plan an extension to the west wing," Richard said. "Do you think you could make a start in designing it before the baby arrives?"

"That is a huge project to attempt."

"It is, but look at this magnificent, sturdy folly you created. Nothing will bring this down; it can withstand whatever the weather throws at it."

Amelia admired the stonework. She was proud of how well the

folly had turned out. "I am not sure this tiny building can compare to a whole new part of the house."

Richard pulled his quizzing glass out of his pocket and, putting it in place, he turned to Amelia. "Are you trying to say that my talented, beautiful wife is not up to the task?"

Laughing, Amelia snatched the quizzing glass and threw it onto the grass. "You and those blasted glasses!"

"I would be far richer if you did not destroy so many."

"And I would be far less tormented if you did not tease me with them constantly."

Richard pulled her onto his knee against her protests of being too heavy. "I must be allowed to provoke you; otherwise, I would just be a besotted fop around you. This way, I can hope to maintain some of my previous reputation."

Shaking her head at her husband, she ran her fingers through his thick, dark hair; she loved that he left it longer these days just so she could do that. "I am afraid it is too late for that. The *ton* despairs at how you fuss around your wife and the way you smile at everyone. I have seen many people disconcerted by the action."

"My wife has corrupted me," Richard groaned.

"And long may it continue," Amelia said, offering him her lips.

The earl took no persuading.

Author's Note

I have had the fortune to live a dream. I've always wanted to write, but life got in the way as it so often does until a few years ago. Then a change in circumstance enabled me to do what I loved: sit down to write. Now writing has taken over my life, holidays being based around research, so much so that no matter where we go, my long-suffering husband says, "And what connection to the Regency period has this building/town/garden got?"

That dream became a little more surreal when in 2018, I became an Amazon StorytellerUK Finalist with Lord Livesey's Bluestocking. A Regency Romance in the top five of an all-genre competition! It was a truly wonderful experience, I didn't expect to win, but I had a ball at the awards ceremony.

I do appreciate it when readers get in touch, especially if they love the characters as much as I do. Those first few weeks after release is a trying time; I desperately want everyone to love my characters that take months and months of work to bring to life.

If you enjoy the books please would you take the time to write a review on Amazon? Reviews are vital for an author, although I admit to bad ones being crushing. Selfishly I want readers to love my stories!

I can be contacted for any comments you may have, via my website:

www.audreyharrison.co.uk

or

facebook.com/AudreyHarrisonAuthor

Please sign-up for email/newsletter—only sent out when there is something to say!

www.audreyharrison.co.uk

You'll receive a free copy of The Unwilling Earl in mobi/epub format for signing-up as a thank you!

About the Author

Audrey lives in the North West of England (a Lancashire Lass) and is of the opinion that she was born about two hundred years too late, especially when dealing with technology! She is a best-selling author of Historical Romance, especially the Regency period.

In the real world she has always longed to write, writing a full manuscript when she was fourteen years old. Work, marriage and children got in the way as they do and it was only when an event at work landed her in hospital that she decided to take stock. One Voluntary Redundancy later, she found that the words and characters came to the forefront and the writing began in earnest.

So, although at home more these days, the housework is still neglected and meals are still late on the table, but she has an understanding family, who usually shake their heads at her and sigh. That is a sign of understanding, isn't it?

Find out more at:
www.audreyharrison.co.uk
or
facebook.com/AudreyHarrisonAuthor
or
Audrey Harrison (@audrey.harrisonauthor) • Instagram photos and videos

Printed in Great Britain
by Amazon